Edward Everett Hale

In His name. A Christmas story

Edward Everett Hale

In His name. A Christmas story

ISBN/EAN: 9783741192012

Manufactured in Europe, USA, Canada, Australia, Japa

Cover: Foto ©Andreas Hilbeck / pixelio.de

Manufactured and distributed by brebook publishing software
(www.brebook.com)

Edward Everett Hale

In His name. A Christmas story

IN HIS NAME.

CHAPTER I.

FÉLICIE.

Félicie was the daughter of Jean Waldo. She was the joy of her father's life, and the joy of the life of Madame Gabrielle, his wife. She was well named Félicie, for she was happy herself and she made everybody happy. She was a sunbeam in the house, in the workshops, in the court-yard, and among all the neighbors. Her father and mother were waked in the morning by her singing; and many a time, when Jean Waldo was driving a hard bargain with some spinner from the country, the mere sight of his pretty daughter as she crossed the court-yard, and the sound of her voice as she sang a scrap of a hymn or of a crusading song, would turn his attention from his barter, and he would relax his hold on the odd sols and deniers as if he had never clung to them. By the same spells she was the joy of the neighborhood. The beggars loved her, the weavers loved her, she could come and go as she chose even among the fullers and dyers, though they were rough fellows, and there was nothing she could not say or do with their wives and children. When the country spinners came in with their yarn, or the weavers with their webs, they would wait, on one excuse or another, really to get a word with her; and many was the rich farm in the valley to which Félicie went in the summer or autumn to make a long visit as she chose. Félicie was queen of her father's household and of all around.

On one of the last days in December, Félicie was making a pilgrimage, after her own fashion, to the church of St. Thomas of Fourvières. The hill of Fourvières is a bold height, rising almost from the heart of the old city of Lyons. And Félicie liked nothing better than a brisk scramble to the top, where, as she said, she might see something. This was her almost daily "pilgrimage." She gave it this name in sport, not irreverent. For, as she went, she always passed by old women who were making a pilgrimage, as they do to this hour, to the church of St. Thomas (now the church of "Our Lady"), which was supposed, and is supposed, to have great power in saving from misfortune those who offer their prayers there. Félicie in passing always looked into the little church, and crossed herself with holy water, and fell on her knees at an altar in a little chapel where was a picture of St. Félicie lying on the ground, wth a vision of Our Lady above. The Félicie who was not a saint would say "Ave Maria" here and "Our Father who art in heaven," and would wait a minute upon her knees, to "see if her father had anything to say to her"; and then would cross herself again, and, as she passed the great altar, would kneel once more, and so would be out in the fresh air again.

This was almost an every-day occurrence. On this day Félicie waited a little longer. Among a thousand votive offerings in the church, hung there by those who were grateful for an answer to their prayers, she saw to-day two which she had never seen before. They were pictures, — not, to tell the truth, very well painted. But to Félicie, the finer or coarser art was a matter of very little account. Each of them represented a scene of preservation in danger. In one of them, a young girl, hardly older than Félicie herself, was to be seen, as she safely floated from a river which bore the ruins of a broken bridge; in the other, a young knight on horseback received unhurt the blows of five terrible Saracens. The Holy Mother could be seen in the clouds with a staff on her arm, turning off the lances of the Paynim. Félicie looked a moment at this picture, but long, very long, at the other.

The disaster which it represented was one which the girl had seen herself, and which had made upon her an impression for her life. Only the year before, Richard the Lion-Hearted and Philip Augustus of France had come to Lyons together, each with a splendid retinue of knights and other soldiers, on their way to the crusade The Archbishop of Lyons was then really an independent prince, and with all the dignity of an independent prince he had received the two kings. There had been much feasting. There had been a splendid ceremony of high mass in the cathedral, and at last, when the two armies had recruited themselves, it was announced that they were to take up their march to the Holy City. Of course all Lyons was on the watch to see the display. Some were in boats upon the river; some were waiting to see them cross the bridge; some walked far out on the road. Girls with flowers threw them before the horse of the handsome English king, and priests in splendid robes carried the banners of the churches and sang anthems as they went. And all Lyons, young and old, was sure that in two or three short months this famous host would be in the City of our Lord!

Alas, and alas! Hardly had the two kings themselves crossed the bridge, and a few of their immediate attendants with them, when, as the great crowd of towns-people pressed in upon the men-at-arms, all eager to see the show, they felt beneath their feet a horrid tremor for one moment, and then — first one length of the bridge, and then, in terrible succession, two others, gave way, and the whole multitude — soldiers, horses, men, women, and children — were plunged into the Rhone below. The torrent was fast, and swept the ruin of timbers and the mass of struggling people and beasts down in horrible confusion. The boatmen on the river did their best to rescue one and another, but were themselves in danger almost equal to that of those who were struggling in the water. The kings turned their horses and rode to the shore, but were as powerless as children to help or even to command And so, in one short hour, this day of glory and of victory was shrouded as in clouds of darkness.

It seemed a miracle, indeed, that only a few were drowned in the chaos; but of those who were rescued, many were maimed for life, and there was not a house in Lyons but had its own tale of danger and suffering.

The picture which Félicie stopped to look at in the church of St. Thomas represented this calamity, and the preservation, by what was called miracle, of Gabrielle L'Estrange, a god-child of Félicie's mother. For herself, Félicie had seen the breaking of the bridge from the safe distance of her eyrie on the mountain. The girl had wisely seen that even her father's good-will could not do much for a child like her in the crowd. She had declared her determination to see the whole; and while others went into the streets to see the armies pass them, Félicie had perched herself on the very top of the hill Fourvières, where she could see every company join in the cortege, where she could hear the blast of music come up to her from the plain.

As she sat here, as the army began to cross the river, the girl had been instantly conscious of the great disaster. She could see the companies in the rear break their ranks and rush towards the stream. She could see the dust of the ruin rise above the river, and could hear the hoarse shouting of people screaming and commanding. She had guessed what the calamity was, and had hurried home to meet only too many stories of personal sorrow. Before night they had known how Gabrielle had been nearly lost, and how she had been saved. And all the mingled memories of that day of glory and of grief came back to Félicie again, now that she saw the picture of her playmate's preservation.

She left the little church, crossing herself again with the holy water, a little more thoughtful than she entered it. The "problem of evil" crossed her mind; and she asked herself why the Virgin should interpose to save Gabrielle, when others were left to perish. But she did not ask this with bitterness. She knew there was answer somewhere. And as she climbed yet higher up the hill, and came out on the glories of her eyrie, the wonders of the winter prospect — more beautiful than ever, as she thought — swept away all memories of death or sorrow or doubt; and the child wrapped her thick shawl round her, as she sat beneath the shelter of a friendly wall, with the full sunlight blazing on her, to wonder for the thousandth time on the beauty of the panorama beyond and below.

There are who say that no view in France can equal it; and I am sure I do not wonder. At her feet the cheerful city lay between the rivers Saone and Rhone, which meet here, just below her. The spires and towers of the cathedral and the churches, even the tallest columns of smoke, as they rose in the still air, were all far, far below the girl on her eyrie. Beyond, she could see at first large farms with their granges, their immense hay-stacks, their barns, and their orchards. She could pick out and name one and another where at the vintage and at harvest she had made pleasant visits this very year. Further, all became brown and purple and blue and gray. Sometimes on a hill she could make out a white church tower, or the long walls of a castle, — just some sign that men and women and happy girls like herself lived there. But Félicie's eye did not rest so long on these. Far above and still beyond — O how far beyond! — was her "old friend," as the girl called Mont Blanc. And to-day he had his rosy face, she said. The sunset behind her was making the snow of the mountain blush with beauty. And nothing can be conceived more dreamy and more lovely than this "vision," as Félicie called it, which even she did not see five times n a year from her eyrie; and which many a lazy canon and abbot, and many a prosperous weaver like her father, and many a thrifty merchant n the town, had never seen at all.

"Good-evening, dear old friend," said the girl, laughing, as if the mountain could hear her ninety miles away, — "good-evening, dear old friend. You are lovely to-night in your evening dress. Will you not come to my Christmas party? Thank you, old friend, for coming out to-night to see me. I should have been very lonely without you, dear old friend. There's a kiss for you! — and there's another! — and there's a feather for you, and there's another!" And she threw into the west wind two bits of down, and pleased herself with watching them as they floated high and quick towards the mountain in the east. "Good-by, dear old friend, good-by. Mamma says I must be home at sunset. Won't you speak to me? — no matter; all the same I know you love me. Good-by! good-by!" And so she tripped down, thinking to herself as she went that everybody and everything did love her, which was very true; thinking that for her, indeed, God's kingdom seemed to have come, and his will to be done on earth as it was in heaven. And the shadow, if it may be called a shadow, of the horrors depicted in the church of St. Thomas was all swept away.

Down she tripped again by the open church, and one after another beggar at the door blessed her as she said, "God bless you." Down she tripped by the convent walls, and wondered how the gardens within world without. And she wondered if the sisters here climbed up the bell tower and looked off on the eastern horizon to see her old friend, and whether they knew how friendly he was to those who loved him. Down she tripped by one zigzag path and another, known to her and to the goats and to none beside; and so, before the sun was fairly down, she had nodded to Pierre the weaver, and had stopped and spoken to Rone the dyer, and had caught up and kissed the twin babies who could hardly tottle along the road, whom Marguerite the wife of young Stephen was leading along; she had said a merry word to half the workmen and half their wives, and had come into the court-yard, and had pushed back the stately heavy oak door, and stood in the hall of Jean Waldo's comfortable house.

Her mother came running out from the kitchen wing to meet the girl. And Félicie ran up to kiss her as she entered, as was her pretty way. And Mistress Gabrielle thought, as she had thought a thousand times, that nobody in the world was as pretty as Félicie, and also that Félicie never had looked as pretty as she did at that very moment. This also had Madam Gabrielle thought a thousand times before. The girl's tightly-fitting tunic was of fine white woollen. But the cape, as in those days the mantle began to be called, also of woollen, was of the brightest scarlet, and, as she had wound it round and round her head, she became a Red Riding-Hood indeed. Her cheeks glowed with life and health as she came running in from the frosty air, and the sharp contrast of her dress was none too bold for a complexion so brilliant. It was the very imper

"Félicie, my child, I have been asking for you. It is St. Victoria's night, you know, and I am giving to them all their Christmas medicine."

"Medicine for me, my dear mother!" And truly the child seemed to need medicine as little as the larks.

"Of course, dear Félicie. Has there been a midsummer or a Christmas since you were born in which I did not give you your medicine? And so is it, thanks to the blessed Virgin and to St. Félicie, that you are so fresh and so well. I have given to your father and to all their men their gentian. I have given to all the women their St. Johnswort, and here is a nice new bottle of the mixture of lavender and rosemary, which I brewed for you when you were away with the Landrys. I have it all waiting."

Félicie knew by long experience that there was no good in argument. Indeed the child was too much used to doing what her mother bade to make argument at any time. This was but a gulp or two of a disagreeable taste, and she knew there would be waiting a honey-cake and an orange after it. So she kissed her mother, ran up-stairs and put away cape and wimple and girdle, and came down-stairs singing: —

My lady came down from her pretty gay room,
In the hall my lady sat down;
Her apron was draped with the roses in bloom,
And her fingers braided a crown, crown, crown!
And her fingers braided a crown!

"But, mamma! how much there is of it. I never had so much before!"

"Darling, you are older now. You have passed your second climacteric." Mistress Gabrielle could be learned when she chose.

"But, mamma, it tastes horridly. It never tasted so badly before."

"Dear child, drink it right down. Here is your orange, to take the taste away. Perhaps it is a little stronger than we have made it. The leaves were the very best I ever saw."

And the dear child made a laughing face of disgust, and then gulped down the bitter mixture as she was bidden.

But then all light faded from her face. With agony such as her mother never saw there, she screamed, "O mamma, dear mamma! — it burns me, it burns me! —you never hurt your darling so before!" And with sobs she could not repress, she hid her face in her mother's bosom, crying out, "O, how it burns, how it burns!"

Mistress Gabrielle was frightened indeed. She tore open the orange, but there was little comfort there. She sent for oils and for snow, and for cold water from the very bottom of the well. But the child's agony seemed hardly checked; and though with a resolute will she would choke down her groans that she might not terrify her mother, it was impossible for her to check the quivering from head to foot, which was a sign of the torture of mouth and throat and stomach. Mistress Gabrielle called for Jeanne and Marie, and they carried the poor child to her bed. They put hot cloths upon her. They warmed her feet and her hands. They made smokes of gums and barks for her to breathe. They tried all the simple and all the complicated arts of the household. One and another neighbor was hurried in, and each contradicted the other, and each advised.

One or other of the more powerful applications would give a moment's relief, but only a moment's. Tears which she could not check would roll down Félicie's cheek to show her inward torture, and that terrible quiver which Mistress Gabrielle learned to dread so horribly would come in with every third or fourth minute. Once and again she had sent for Jean Waldo, her husband. But none of the lads could find him. Night had closed dark around them, and he did not return. It was then that she took the responsibility which she had never taken before, and sent for the young Florentine doctor, whose shop, next the cathedral, attracted the wonder and superstition of all the neighborhood. "Bid him come, Adrian, on the moment! Tell him that my daughter is dying, and that he has not a moment to lose. For the love of Christ, beg him to come on the instant." Dying! The word struck new terror in the whole panic-swayed household. Everybody had been in distress, but no one had dared think or say that the darling of them all, but just now so strong and so happy, could die! Least of all had Mistress Gabrielle permitted herself to think it. But now all her pride was gone. Niobe before Apollo was not more prostrate. She knew that if the Florentine was to render any help, it must be rendered right soon. And so, with a calmness of despair at which she wondered herself, she sent word to him that her daughter was dying.

CHAPTER II.

JEAN WALDO.

Giulio, the Florentine doctor, came up the street with the boy who had been sent for him, and with a blackamoor who bore a great hamper which contained his medicines and his instruments. As they rapidly approached the doorway they overtook Jean Waldo himself, slowly walking up the street. Till they spoke to him, the father was wholly unconscious of the calamity which had fallen on his child.

If you had told Jean Waldo that afternoon, as he sat in the Treasurer's seat at the guild-meeting, that, in after times, his name of Waldo would be best known to all people, in all lands, because his kinsman, Pierre Waldo, bore it, he would have been much amazed, and would have taken you for a fool. Kinsmen they were, there was no doubt of that. Nobody could look on their faces — nay, even on their eyes or their beards, or on the shape of their hands or their finger-nails, and not see that there was near kindred between them. "We are both from the valley of Vaud," Jean Waldo used to say when people questioned him. But he was not pleased to have them question him. He had taken good care not to mix himself up with Pierre Waldo's heresies. "Why does he want to trouble himself about the priests?" said Jean Waldo. "Why does he not do as I do? I take care of myself, and I let other people take care of themselves. Why cannot Pierre Waldo, my kinsman, if he is my kinsman, do as I do?"

prosperous way. He squeezed down the spinners who brought yarn to him. He squeezed the weavers who brought him webs. He kept a good company of the best workmen, bleachers and dyers, in his own workshops, and he had near forty looms of his own, with his own weavers. He put up linen cloths for market more neatly and handsomely, the traders said, than any man in Lyons, and so he prospered exceedingly. "This is what comes," he said, "of minding your own business, and letting other people's business alone."

Pierre Waldo, the kinsman of whom Jean spoke with such contempt, and who is now remembered in all the world where the Christian religion is known, had been a prosperous merchant in Lyons. But Pierre Waldo was not one of those who went to mass only because the priests bade him. He went to the mass because God had been good to him and to his, and he wanted to express his thanks He was glad to express thanks as other people did and where they did.' He had always had a passion for reading, for in his boyhood his mother had taught him to read. And when, one day, a parchment book came in his way, which proved to be an Evangelistary, or copy of the Four Gospels, in Latin, Pierre Waldo began to try to read this, and with wonder and delight which cannot be told. Father John of Lugio, the priest whom he knew best, an honest man and an humble priest, was willing to help Pierre as he could about the Latin. And there was not so much difference in those days between Latin and the Romance language which half Pierre Waldo's customers used, that he should find it hard to make out the language in which the book was written that so excited him. When Father John saw how much pleasure Pierre Waldo took in such reading, he was glad to show to him, in the church and in the vestry, other parchments, in which were Paul's letters and the Book of the Revelation. And at last Pierre had seen the whole of the Old Testament also, and he and the good priest had read some parts of the Old Law.

Who shall say whether this knowledge of the Bible could ever have come to anything with Pierre Waldo, but for a terrible incident which made its mark on his whole life? He and the other merchants of his section of the town used to meet each other very often at little feasts, in which they showed their hospitality and wealth at the same time, in the elegance of the service, the richness of the food, and in the choice of the good old wine. A party of them were together one night at such a feast in the house of Robert the Gascon. They had eaten a hearty supper. The wine had passed freely, and one of the company, a favorite with all of them, had sung a love song such as the romances of the day were full of. The glasses clattered in the applause, and one and another of the guests bade him sing it again. But for some reason Walter, the singer, declined. The moment he said "No," William Jal, an old and near friend of Pierre Waldo, who was sitting at his side at the table, rose and said, with a loud laugh, "You shall sing it, Walter!" And he brought his fist down on the table, and with this terrible oath he went on,—

"By God, you shall sing it, Walter, or I will never taste wine again!"

Hardly had the awful words left

his mouth when the expression of his face changed in sudden agony. He seemed to try to balance himself at the table for an instant, and then fell dead upon the floor.

From that moment Pierre Waldo was a new man. In the night of horror which followed this scene of mockery and revel, in his wretched efforts to comfort the widow to whom they carried the cold corpse home, and the poor children who were waked from their beds to look upon it, — in that night of horror Pierre Waldo had chance to look forward and to look backward. And he did so. From that time forward his reading of the Gospel was no mere literary amusement. He copied it for his own use; he translated it for his neighbors' use. He found that other men, anxious and pious, had already felt as he began to feel, — that all the people had a right to parable, to psalm, and to the words of the blessed Master. One after another of his customers brought him, from one and another town where they travelled, bits of Paul or Matthew or Luke which had been translated into the vulgar language. Pierre Waldo's home and his warehouse became the centre of those who sought a purer and simpler life. For himself, after that dreadful night with the fatherless children and their mother, Pierre Waldo said he would give all he had to the poor. Whoever was in need in Lyons or in the country round came to him for advice and for help, and they gained it. If they came for food, they had food — always they found a friend.

Almost all the company of merchants who were with Pierre on that night joined him in this service of those that were in need. The company of them began to be called, and called themselves, the "Poor Men of Lyons." They had no new religion. Their religion was what they found in the Saviour's words to the young nobleman, to Peter the fisherman, and to Mary Magdalene. And so taken were they with these words, that they read them to all who came for help to them, and were eager to copy them out in the people's language, and give the copies to all who would carry them into the country.

Almost at the same time, Francisco of Assisi was moved in much the same way to give up all he had to the poor, and to preach the gospel of poverty. If these two men had come together! But it does not appear that they ever heard each other's names.

No! At that time Lyons was governed wholly by the great religious corporation which was known as the Chapter of St. John, under the Archbishop, who was in fact a Prince, and as a Prince governed the city and the country at his will. When he found that the merchants were entering on the business of distributing the Scriptures and reading them to the people, the Archbishop and the Chapter forbade it. The "Poor Men of Lyons" must leave that business to the clergy.

Pierre and his friends were amazed. They went to the Holy Father at Rome, and told him what their work was. He was well pleased with it, gave them his approval, but told them they must not preach without the permission of the Archbishop and Chapter. This permission those great men would not grant to the "Poor Men." They refused it squarely.

Refused permission to make the words of the Lord Jesus known! It was at this point that Pierre Waldo and the Poor Men of Lyons broke away from the priests and the Pope. "They have abandoned the faith," he said; "and we ought to obey God rather than man."

This was the signal on which the Archbishop and the Chapter drove Pierre Waldo out from Lyons, and all those who followed him. His house and his warehouses, all his books that they could find, they seized, and he and his had to take flight into the mountains.

This was the reason why the prosperous Jean Waldo, the master-weaver, the father of the pretty Félicie, was not well pleased when men asked him if he and Pierre Waldo were kinsmen or no. He did not want to be mixed up with any "Poor Men of Lyons." Not he. He was not one of the poor men of Lyons, and he did not mean to be. Pierre Waldo was in a good business, he said; there was not a merchant in Lyons with better prospects before him, when he took up with his reading and writing, his beggars, his ministers, and all the rest of their crew. And so Jean Waldo would come out, again and again, with his favorite motto: "I take care of myself, let them take care of themselves. If Pierre would have stuck to his own business, he would not be hiding in the mountains there."

Such was the man who, as he slowly walked up the hill just now, thought himself above all need of asking a service from any man in this world. He would not have recognized Giulio the Florentine this very afternoon, if they had passed each other, though he knew the man's face perfectly well. If you had asked him why he did not salute such a man, or even show a consciousness of his existence, Jean Waldo would have said, —

"I take care of myself; let the Florentine take care of himself. My business is not his, and his is not mine."

But now, as has been said, in the narrow street, the Florentine and his servant, and the boy Adrian, who had been sent to summon him in hot haste, overtook the dignified master-weaver, as he walked home slowly and complacently. It was with no little difficulty that Jean Waldo was made to understand that his treasure and delight, his own Félicie, who only at dinner-time had been so happy and so lovely, was dying, or seemed to be dying, in the home he left so little while before.

After this it was not Jean Waldo who walked slowly in that party. He seized the great basket which the black servant bore, and fairly compelled him in his energy to go faster. He poured question upon question out as to what had happened upon the Florentine, who was of course wholly unable to answer him. And thus the breathless party arrived together, under the heavy archway of the courtyard of Jean Waldo's house.

CHAPTER III.

THE FLORENTINE.

The young physician whom Madame Gabrielle had summoned to the rescue, was a native of the city of Florence, and he had not been so long a resident of Lyons but that he was still called "the Florentine." At that time the profession of a physician, as a distinct calling among men, was scarcely known. The clergy were expected to know something of the cure of disease, and in some instances they really attained remarkable skill in its treatment.

But with the knowledge of eastern art which had come in with the first and second crusades, and with the persistent study of those naturalists whom we call alchemists, a wider and more scientific knowledge of the human frame and its maladies was beginning to take the place of old superstitions and other delusions. And thus it happened that here and there was a man who, without being a priest on the one hand or a barber on the other, had gained the repute of understanding disease and of the power of keeping death at bay. Such a man was Giulio the Florentine.

He moved quickly and with a decided step. He spoke little, and always after a moment's pause, if he were questioned. It seemed as if he spoke by some sort of machinery, which could not be adjusted without an instant's delay. What he said was crisp and decided, as were his steps in walking. It was impossible to see his manner, even of crossing the room, or of arranging his patient's head upon the pillow, without feeling confidence in him. "I felt as if there were a prophet in the house," said Mathilde, one of the maid-servants, who had been sent for hot water into the kitchen, and in that minute took occasion to repeat her hasty observations to the excited party assembled there.

When he entered the sick-room, it was more than an hour after Félicie had drained to the bottom the beaker which Madame Gabrielle had filled full of the bitter decoction. The burning pain of the first draught had passed away or had been relieved by some of the palliatives which had been given. But the second stage was if possible more terrible than that of the agony of the beginning. On the pretty bed where they had laid her, in the chamber which the child had decorated with the various treasures which she had acquired in her wanderings, she would lie for a few minutes as if insensible, and then would spring up in the most violent convulsions. She threw herself from side to side without knowing any of those who tried to soothe her, and who were forced to hold her. A few minutes of this violence would be followed by renewed insensibility which seemed almost as terrible.

Just after one of these paroxysms, her mother was wiping away the frothy blood which burst from the poor child's nostrils, when the Florentine entered the room. She made place for him, in a moment, by the bed; and, with that firm hand of the prophet, which struck Mathilde with such awe, he felt his patient's forehead and then the pulse in her wrist. Then he examined, one by one, the simples which the mother and her neighbors had been administering by way of emetic and of antidote. From his own hamper, with the aid of the blackamoor, he supplied the places of these with tinctures — of which the use in medicine was then almost wholly new — of which he knew the force, and on the results of which he could rely. He applied and continued the external applications which the eager women were making to the poor child's body.

But having noted, in about two minutes, who of these various assistants had a head, and never spoke, he then banished from the room, with a kind dignity that nothing could resist, all the others, except the poor mother. He crossed to the window, and, though the night was so cold, he admitted a breath of the winter air. Then he came back to the bedside, and, with the courtesy of a monarch, asked Madame to tell him all she could of the tragedy. With the courtesy of a monarch he listened to her rambling story, still keeping his hand on the forehead or on the pulse of his patient. Madame Gabrielle, with the tears running down her cheeks, plunged into the account of what had happened; and to all she said he gave careful heed, never once attempting to check her, even in the wildest excursions which she made to the right or to the left, — into "*dit-elle*" and *dit-il* and "*je disais*," — "says he" and "says she" and "says I." He seemed to know that with all her tackings, even if she "missed stays" sometimes, she would come by her own course best to her voyage's end.

It was not till this whole story was over that he asked to see the diet-drink, as Madame called it, which had worked all this misery. But at that moment, his poor patient started in another spasm of these terrible convulsions.

Then was it that the balance and steadiness of the "prophet" showed itself as it had not shown itself till now. He seemed to control even her almost by a word, as none of the chattering or beseeching of those whom he had sent away had done. When he held her, he held her indeed, so that she did not even struggle against his grasp; when he bade her open her mouth to swallow the sedative which the black brought him at his direction, the poor delirious child obeyed him as she would obey a God; and under such control the crisis passed, her mother said, much more easily and quickly than that of half an hour before. Still there was the same bloody froth upon her lips and nostrils, there was the same deadly pallor as of a corpse; and the haggard aspect which came at once over the face seemed to Madame Gabrielle and her two waiting women more terrible than ever. The Florentine noted the pulse again, as the exhausted child sank back, and counted the rapidity of her breathing. Then for the first time he began his examination of the poison.

He tasted it, once and again, as fearlessly as if it had been water or wine. If he were puzzled, or if he were distressed by what he learned, he did not show it in any glance of those black eyes, or in the least change of any other feature. He turned to Madame Gabrielle again to ask her when it was brewed, and where she had obtained the materials.

The answer was as voluble as before, and was not, alas, very helpful. The good dame's custom, for years upon years, — ever since she was a married woman indeed, — had been to go on St. John's Day and on St. Margaret's Day and on the Eve of the Assumption and on Halloween, to collect the various ingredients which were necessary for the different home medicines of a household so large as hers. Rosemary, wild lavender, Mary's lavender, tansey, rue, herb-saffron, herb-dittany, motherwort, spearwort, maid's wort, and St. John's wort, herb of heaven, herb of winter, poison-kill, and feverfew, she named them all glibly. And if the expert shuddered within as he thought of the principles which were hidden under these names, repeated so recklessly by an ignorant woman, he did not show his anger or vexation And this year, as usual, she said she had gone out on the Eve of St. John's day, — surely he knew that spearwort and herb-of-heaven and herb-dittany were never so strong as when you gathered them on the Eve of St. John's Day, if the moon were at the full, — and again she went out, with the two bay horses on the St. Margaret's Day at e'en, and came back with three large baskets full of simples. So she did on Assumption Eve. But when it came to Halloween she confessed that she was kept at home, watching the conservation of some peaches. The accident — for accident of course there was — must have happened then. She had sent out Goodwife Prudhon, who certainly ought to know. If any one knew anything about the simples of the valley, it was Goodwife Prudhon. It was she who brought in the bark and the roots of the autumn, which the dame herself had not collected. And for the brewing itself — O! that was on St. Elizabeth's Day and St. Cecile's Day. The posset indeed was mixed of decoctions which were not six weeks old.

Could she bring him any of the roots or bark which Madame Prudhon brought her, or had she used them all?

O! Madame Gabrielle was quite sure she had not used them all; and she retired, to search for what might be left, to her own sanctuary, not sorry, perhaps, thus to avoid for the moment the presence of her wretched husband. He had been sent away from the room on some errand which had been made for him by the ingenuity of the Florentine, and it was only at this moment that he returned.

So in poor Félicie's next paroxysm of convulsions it was Jean Waldo who obeyed the Florentine's orders. And in that crisis the Florentine took his measure also, and learned what manner of man he was. The father was as firm as the physician. He knew his place too, and he obeyed every direction to a letter. It was piteous to see how he sought for a recognition from his daughter, which she would not give. But whether he hoped or despaired, the poor man could obey. He brought what the Florentine bade him bring. He stood where he bade him stand. With a hand as firm as the physician's, he dropped the drops of the sedative from the silver flask in which it was kept. And with a hand and arm as steady, he supported the pillow on which she was to fall back after she had taken it. The paroxysm was shorter and less vehement than those before it. But it seemed to be checked, rather from the exhaustion of the patient, than from any relaxation of the disease. Jean Waldo himself knew that flesh and blood could not long abide racking so terrible.

As she sank back to rest, the Florentine counted her pulsations and the rate of her breathing as carefully as he did before. He took from his pocket a silver ball, opened it by a screw, and drew from the interior a long silken cord, one end of which was attached to it. At the other end was a small silver hook, and this the Florentine fastened high in the curtains of the room opposite to where he was sitting. He had thus made a pendulum, several ells in length, and he set it to swinging solemnly.

He returned to the child's bedside, and with his hand upon her heart noted the wiry, stubborn pulsations, and compared their number with the vibrations of the ball he had set in motion. Once and again he bade Jean Waldo strike the ball for him, when its original motion was in part exhausted.

While they were thus occupied, poor Madame Gabrielle, the guilty or guiltless author of so much wretchedness, returned. Her apron was full of herbs, barks, powders, and roots, tied up in separate parcels, and each parcel carefully labelled. The Florentine took them, one by one, tasted each, and made a note of the name of each, the blackamoor holding his inkhorn for him that he might do so. The mother by this time was awed into silence, and never spoke till she was spoken to; but when she was asked, she was confident in her replies. They were able without the least doubt to lay out upon the table the bark, the two parcels of leaves, and the white roots which had been steeped and soaked, boiled and brewed, in the preparation of the "diet-drink."

As if he had to adjust his speaking apparatus with a little "click," or as if he disliked to speak at all, the Florentine said to the father and the mother, "Here was the good-wife Prudhon's blunder. She thought that she had here the root of Spanish maiden-wort. She did not see the leaves; I suppose they had dried up and were gone. But it is the root of hemlock-leaved œnanthe, what the peasants call snake-bane. Juba, bring me the parcel of œnanthè." He showed to the father and mother that good-wife Prudhon's maiden-wort was, in fact, the most dreaded poison in his repertory.

"And is there no antidote?" asked the father, so eagerly!

"The antidote," said the physician, kindly, "is to do what your wife has tried to do, — to throw out from the dear child's body what by such misfortune has been put in." And he said one word to comfort the poor blunderer. "Well for her that she was at home, and that her mother was at hand." Then he added reverently, "God only knows how much is left in her stomach of this decoction; but she drank enough of it to have killed us all, had not her mother's promptness compelled her stomach to throw off the most part of the poison."

And this was all that he seemed disposed to say. The father and the mother were both in too much awe of him to dare to question him. With the lapse of every half-hour he would bid one or the other of them set his silver pendulum in motion, and he would note carefully the pulse of the girl, entering on his note-book a memorandum of his observation. But neither Jean Waldo nor his wife dared ask if there were improvement or decline. He renewed from time to time the applications which had been made to the child's feet and legs and stomach. From time to time she started again in the terrible convulsions. But these were shorter and shorter, and more and more infrequent, either from the power of his medicines, or from some change in the action of the poison. Jean Waldo thought that the physician regarded the reaction from the paroxysm as more alarming than the struggle itself. But who could tell what that man of iron thought, or did not think; felt, or did not feel? The poor father knew that very probably he was but imagining that the Florentine showed his own anxieties. And who was he to ask him?

At midnight the girl started up in one of these spasms of agony; and at this time she spoke with more connection of ideas than any of them had been able to trace before: "This way! this way! Gabrielle, dear Gabrielle, do you not hear me, my child? It is Félicie, — your own pet, Gabrielle! Never fear! never fear! I have spoken to Our Mother, to Our Lady, you know! That is brave — my own little cousin, that is brave. Care! Care! See that heavy timber! O how good! O how good! She is quite right, quite right. All safe, all safe, all safe" And as she sighed out these words, she rested from the most violent and passionate exertion, as if she had been hard at work in some effort, which the Florentine did not in the least understand.

It was the first time that he ever seemed to make any inquiry regarding her symptoms, and he looked his curiosity rather than expressed it. Madame Waldo was relieved at having a fair opportunity to speak. "Gabrielle is her cousin, my sister Margaret's oldest daughter, if you please. Félicie is fond — O so fond — of Gabrielle. And she thinks Gabrielle is in danger, O yes! O yes! See, she thinks the bridge is breaking, and that Gabrielle is in the water. Your reverence remembers, perhaps, that the Holy Mother saved Gabrielle and so many more when the bridge went down." But by this time the physician, only bowing civilly as he acknowledged her voluble explanations, was counting the pulse-beats again, and by a motion directed Jean Waldo to renew the vibration of the pendulum.

Was he perhaps a little more satisfied with his count and comparison than he had been before? Who can tell? for none of the four attendants in the darkened room dared to ask him.

And then he sent Jean Waldo away. The wretched father begged that he might stay, but the Florentine was as flint. Madame Gabrielle and one of her maids would give him all the assistance he wanted besides what his own man could render him, and more. Indeed, he would send her away also, he said, in an aside, but that he knew it would kill her to go. At last he pitied the poor beseeching father so much that he promised to let him come in, an hour before day-break, and take his wife's place at the bedside of his child. Jean Waldo went because he was bidden. His strong, selfish will gave way before the strong, unselfish will of this stranger. Prophet indeed! This prophet worked the miracle of commanding Jean Waldo, and he saw that he obeyed him.

Long before it was light, however, the heart-broken father, who had slept not a wink in the dreary hours between, came to claim the right of taking his turn. And now he and the Florentine sent Madame Gabrielle away, weak as she now was from her wretchedness and her watching and her anxiety. Yes! The night had given but little of encouragement. The paroxysms of convulsion were, it is true, more and more seldom; but the prostration after them was more and more terrible. It seemed too clear now to the mother that the child was too weak for nature to rally from the struggle of the paroxysm. Nor did she in the least regain her consciousness. The black features and strange look of the servant did not surprise her, nor did her mother's familiar face call the least look of recognition. In the intervals of rest, her rest was absolute. She saw nothing, said nothing, and seemed to hear nothing then. When she roused to these horrid battles the delusion was now one thing and now another. She saw the sinking bridge, or she was talking to some lame beggar woman, so fast that they could hardly catch her words, or she was throwing kisses and waving her hand to her dear mountain far away, or she was running down the side of the Hill of Fourvières that she might be sure to arrive at home in time to meet her father when she came down to supper. In these delusions the wise physician humored her. But she seemed to have no knowledge of him nor of any of them, nor any consciousness of their presence. The phantoms before her were all she saw or heard. And they vanished as strangely and as suddenly as they came. In the midst of one of these quick harangues to them, she would sink back on the pillow, which the black held ready for her, as if she were too completely exhausted and prostrate with the exertion to utter another syllable.

It was just after one of these visions, and the paroxysm accompanying it, that Jean Waldo returned, and that his wife was sent away. It seemed that the resolute man had been nursing resolution in his night-watch in the passage-way, and that he was resolved to know the best or the worst; that he would command the young man to tell him all that he could tell him. He set the pendulum in motion as he was bidden; he filled with hotter water a jar for the child's feet to rest upon, and exchanged for it that which was on the bed; he spread the napkin at her mouth, as the Florentine fed her from an elixir, which, as Jean Waldo saw, was not the same which they used at midnight. Then when she rested and all was still, he said, firmly, —

"Tell me the worst, sir. Is the child dying or living? I am not a fool."

The Florentine looked up and said, after the moment of preparation, "If I thought you were a fool, you would not be in the room with my patient. You know all that I know, because you have eyes to see. These paroxysms of agony are less frequent. The last interval was nearly twice as long as the first was, I should think. She is wholly free from pain too, and her pulse, though it beats so quick, beats with a more reasonable edge than when I came in. But her strength is failing all the same. Her breath is quicker; and if the interval is longer, it is because nerve and muscle and life, whatever that is, cannot rally to the struggle as they did in the evening. She is at the omnipotent age, and her life has been strong and pure as an angel's. Were it not for that she would have been dead before now." And the silent man paused, but paused as if he would like to say something more.

For this "something more" the distressed father waited; he thought he waited an eternity, but it did not come. "Can you not say anything more?" he said, miserably. "What is it that we are doing? What are these elixirs and tisans? Is not there somewhere in God's world, some potion — do you not call it an antidote — which will put out this poison as water puts out fire?"

"Is there not? Is there?" said the Florentine, setting the click of his talking apparatus more resolutely if possible than before. "If there is, the wit of man has not discovered it. How should it? The water which puts out the fire is the same water which drowns the sailor. For aught you and I can tell, this root, of which the decoction seemed liquid flame when your daughter drank it, may give life itself to some fish or beast or bird for which the good God made it. All that we do, my friend," — it was the first time he had used those words in that house, — "all that we do is to undo what we did wrong before. We have tried to rid her system of this wretched decoction, and now we are trying to give time, whatever that is; and nature, whatever that is; and life, whatever that is, — the chance to do their perfect work. We can do nothing more. The good God wishes and means to save health and strength and joy and abundant life. So much we know; and knowing that, in the strength and life of a pure child of His, like this girl, we hope, and have a right to hope."

"Is this all?" said the father sadly, after another pause, in which he thought the Florentine wanted to say more. "Is this all? What is the tisan, what is the mustard on her stomach, what is the rubbing, what is the hot water at her feet, what is the elixir in your phial?"

"Ah well!" replied the expert, after a longer pause than usual perhaps, in what seemed like the adjustment of his machinery; "what is it indeed? It is our poor effort to quicken and help from the outside the processes of this nature which is so mysterious in the beautiful machine. The hot water at her feet keeps them more near to the warmth which nature gives. My master taught me that when the foot and arm and leg are fully warm, each movement of the heart drove easily a tide of the blood of life itself through them all. You can see that the warmth of the jar should make that process easier for this poor heart which finds its work so hard. Ah well! it seems as if we helped it more by the friction of these cloths, so long as we do not annoy her by it, and as if these sinapisms wrought in the same way. We think we know that within her system tinctures which we have tried give the same help to a life which is too weak. Perhaps they enable some part of her nervous system which the poison has not reached to act for the good of the part that it first affected."

Then the talking apparatus seemed to fail the expert. He opened his mouth once and again; he then said "I" once or twice, but seemed to reconsider his determination, and to determine that he would add nothing more.

"But we are so well, and she is so faint there. Is it not strange that I cannot give her of this fresh blood of mine, or from my life, five years, ten, twenty? I would give them gladly."

"Ah, my friend," said the expert, without a moment's pause this time; "do not speak as if we gave anything or did anything. It is God gives, and God who takes. All that you and I can do is so to adjust and so to relieve, and perhaps so to help, this poor frail machine, that the breath of life God gave it may be able to work His work. You would give your life for hers, I do not doubt it. For one, I would have given my life once for the brother who was dearest to me. My master opened the vein which you see scarred here, and with a silver tube he drew the healthy, fresh blood from my young life into the failing veins of his ebbing life. But it could not be, my friend," he added, after another long pause. "His life was his, and mine was mine. Perhaps in another world our lives may be closer, and we may be made perfect in one." It seemed as if this confidence with the father broke some spell which had been on the adept's tongue before. He sat still for a few minutes, with his hand upon the girl's heart, then rose and went round the bed, and at her back listened for her breath, and felt again the heat of his water jugs. Then as he resumed his seat, he said, half aloud: —

"I wish my master were here!" It was the first wish he had expressed, the first intimation that he and his horrid blackamoor and the great hamper could not produce everything which human wit could suggest in the exigency.

Jean Waldo jumped eagerly at the suggestion.

"Your master? Who is he, where is he? Let me send, let me go, let me beg him to come. Will money buy him? Here is enough of that! What are gold and silver to me, if this child die?"

"Has not this night taught you, sir, that life is something that men cannot buy or sell?" The adept spake if possible more proudly than ever. "Know, sir, the reason why my master was not first at this child's bedstead, with all his skill and tenderness and experience. It is because he cared for the Poor Men of Lyons, more than the Rich men of Lyons."

Then there came one of those queer clicks in his talking machinery, as if he were too indignant to say more. But he went on: —

"Your priests yonder, with their bells and their masses, and their feasts inside their convents; your famous chapter and your famous abbot could not bear to have the 'Poor Men of Lyons' fed or taught, and so they drove my master away, and your kinsman away, and you know how many others. Men say and I believe that it was because these men knew Holy Scripture better than they knew it, and because they loved the poor better than they loved them. This is certain, that these men went about doing good, that they fed the hungry and gave drink to the thirsty, they took the stranger into their homes and they ministered to the sick and those that were in prison, they brought glad tidings to the poor and comfort to those in sorrow. I do not know much of Holy Scripture, but I always supposed that this was the Pure Gospel. It was not pure enough for your priests, and so the liege lords of Lyons drove those men away. That is the reason why my master is not at your daughter's bedside."

The young physician stopped short, as if he had let his indignation run further than was wise. A wretched feeling, a sickness at heart swept over Jean Waldo, when he remembered how often he had said to these men who were in exile with his kinsman, that they would have been wiser to have minded their own business. Of his kinsman himself he had said, once and again, "If he would only mind his own concerns, all would be well." Now Jean Waldo began to see that he did want some one to take care of him and his, and that this grand selfishness of his was only fitted for the times of high prosperity.

"Is your master beyond all recall?" he said, a dim notion crossing his mind that he had heard some of the rich burghers say that the "Poor Men of Lyons" were hiding in the mountains.

"I have not seen my master there," replied the Florentine, thoughtfully "His home is in the Brevon caves, among men who have never betrayed him, beyond Cornillon and St. Rambert."

"St. Rambert," said the father, eagerly,—"St. Rambert,—it is close to us, a miserable six hours away. I have horses in these stables that would take me there in six hours."

The adept looked uneasily at the child, when her father spoke of six hours, as if he would say, "And where will she be when six hours only are gone?" But he did not say this. He said, "My master is not at Cornillon, he is in the valley of the Brevon beyond. Still, as you say, that is not so far away."

"Send for him! send for him!" cried the father; "send for him if you have one ray of hope!" And the eagerness both of his attitude and his voice would have moved a harder listener than the Florentine. It seemed as if the child herself was conscious of what passed. She moved her head a little on the pillow and a sunny smile floated over her face, the first expression except that of agony or anxiety which the adept had seen there.

"If you will send, I will write," said the adept; and he whispered to the black, who brought to him from a case in the hamper a strip of vellum already folded for a letter.

"Have you a trusty man whom you can send with this? Bid your grooms saddle the horse, — and he needs to be your best, — while I am writing.

Jean Waldo asked nothing more but to be doing something, and at the word left the room.

The Florentine wrote : —

"Here is a child dying because she has drunk a decoction of hemlock-leaved œnanthe. I think there was also the milky blush mushroom or the Picardy peaussière in the decoction. Come if you can help us.

For the love of Christ.

GIULIO."

And in the middle, at the bottom, he drew with some little care the symbol known as the Cross of Malta.

He added, "We have no moment to lose. Before day-break of St. Ives."

Meanwhile the father had hurried down the dark passages, out into the court-yard, past the workshops to the room where Hugh Prinhac, the most resolute of the weavers, slept; a man who in street fights had again and again led the weavers' apprentices in their victories over the dyers.

He knocked at the door, and knocked again and again till he heard a motion within. To a gruff "Who's there?" he gave his name in reply; and in an instant the astonished journeyman threw the door open for his master.

"Prinhac, my daughter is dying. The only man that can save her is this Italian, who is only five hours away. Prinhac, as you love me, take this parchment, and bring him."

Prinhac was but half awake perhaps. The enterprise was not attractive, nor did it seem as if his employer counted very wisely when he relied on such love as the weaver bore him. Prinhac asked some hesitating question.

"For the love of Christ, do not stay to argue," said the poor old man.

Without knowing it, he struck a chord in using the sacred words, and in an instant the weaver was ready for any duty. "Who stays to argue?" said he. "Do you see that your black stallion is saddled, and by the time the horse is here, I will be ready to mount. Love of Christ indeed! And who says I tarry when I am invoked IN HIS NAME?"

CHAPTER IV.

UP TO THE HILLS.

SURE enough, the weaver stood on the step of the door, booted and spurred, when the trembling old man appeared with his lantern leading out Barbe-Noire from the low gateway of the mews. It was long since Jean Waldo had saddled and bridled a horse for himself, but he had not forgotten the arts of his boyhood, and the Arab needed no care because his master was his groom. At the same moment Giulio the Florentine appeared from above, and as Prinhac mounted promptly, Giulio put his hand over the mane of the horse, and almost in a whisper, though they three were all alone in the night, he gave the young fellow precise directions where and how Lugio was to be found. Prinhac bent in the saddle, listened carefully, and repeated the directions to be sure that he had not mistaken them.

"Never fear me, then!" he said, spurred his horse, and was away.

"He must cross the bridge before sundown," cried poor Jean Waldo to the rider, himself startled as he remembered how narrow was the range thus given.

"Never fear," was still the cheerful answer, and Prinhac disappeared into the night.

The ride across the narrow peninsula which parts the Saone from the Rhone, and is to-day covered by the most beautiful part of the city of Lyons, took but a few minutes,—and the rider was soon at the long, narrow bridge over the larger river, which had been temporarily constructed, by the direction of Richard of the Lion Heart, after the ruin of the year before. "The old man bids us return before sunset. He has forgotten that I have started before sunrise." This was the thought which amused Prinhac so that even a smile curled over his hard face as he rode up to the gateway of the bridge.

The truth was, that no passage was permitted before sunrise, under the sharp orders of the Viguier. But many things were done in the priest-governed city of Lyons, which neither Viguiers nor Seneschals nor Couriers nor the Chapter nor the Bishop suspected. And this the reader will see.

"Hola! Who commands the guard?" cried Prinhac. "Turn out! Turn out! Is this the way our bridges are watched?"

A sleepy sentinel appeared.

"Hola! who commands the guard?" cried the fearless weaver again.

"And what is that to you?" replied the sentinel, throwing his halberd forward in carte. "If you see the guard, it ought to be enough for you."

Prinhac did not stop to argue. But the sentinel, as he watched him in the dim lantern-light, saw that he made in the air the sign of a Maltese Cross, and heard him say, in a low whisper, "Send me the officer of the guard

IN HIS NAME."

Sign and whisper were enough. The sentry threw up his halberd in a military salute and was gone. Nor did the rider wait a minute in the cold, before the officer of the guard, fully dressed in armor, passed out from the gateway and saluted.

"Can you let me pass, Mr. Officer?" said Prinhac, quietly and modestly this time. "It is *for the Love of Christ* that I am riding."

"Go —

IN HIS NAME,"

Was the only reply made to the weaver. The officer turned, passed into the guard-house, and, as if by invisible hand, the portcullis rose before Prinhac, the only bar to his passage, and in a moment he was on the bridge. The grate fell behind him, and he was again alone.

"And how would my master have passed there?" he said to himself, half aloud. And the same grim smile crept over his face, — "he should have asked his friend the Bishop, or our distinguished boon companion the Seneschal, to give him a pass that he might send into the mountains for the doctor they have driven away." And then aloud, "Hist, hist, Barbe-Noire! You are not at Chateaudun; this is no race-course. You shall have running enough before to-day is over. But in the dark, over these rotten boats, you must step more carefully, my beauty."

And so the rough fellow began musing on the strange chance which had put him astride this horse, which, in the judgment of weavers, spinners, fullers, and dyers, of the whole of the little community indeed which found its centre in Jean Waldo's court-yard, — was by far the noblest horse in Lyons. Nor were they far from right in their judgment. The noble creature had first appeared there when Jean Waldo rode him back from a long absence in Marseilles. What price he had paid, or what debts he had forgiven for him, no man in the workshops knew. But there were rumors as to the wild life of the merchant who had been his last owner, and of fight with the Barbary corsair who had been his master before. How these things might be, Prinhac did not know. He did know that any groom who was permitted to cross Barbe-Noire's saddle for an hour, would brag for a week of that honor, and that, for his own part, he might the morning before as well have wished for the crown of Burgundy, as to have wished for the permission to ride Barbe-Noire for a day.

And so the weaver was led on, as the horse took surer foothold on the causeway, to ask himself why his master chose him from all workmen for this mission. Lucky for Jean Waldo, the man thought it, that he chose as he did. "Which of them would have seen that portcullis rise, as I did?" Ah, Prinhac, Prinhac! perhaps more of them have the talisman than you think for!

The truth was that when the Bishop John Fine-House, — Jean des Belles Maisons, as some of the archives call him, — when John Fine-House, I say, or John Fine-Hands, as others call him, chose to banish Peter Waldo and the "Poor Men of Lyons" from his city, he strained his new-bought authority more harshly than he knew. When the Archbishop and Chapter had refused to the Poor Men of Lyons the right to assemble in the public places, or indeed anywhere, to read the gospels, they had themselves possessed for only six years what they had long wished for, the temporal government of the city and outlying country. Before the Pope of Rome had any such power in Rome, the Archbishop of Lyons was as good as an independent Prince in Lyons. In 1173 the Count of Forez and his son had sold out all their rights there, in exchange for some lands owned by the Chapter, and eleven hundred marks of money. The rulers of Burgundy had too little to do with such "Counties" to interfere, and practically the Archbishop found himself a sovereign prince. The town of Lyons became his fief, and all the administration was in his name.

One of his first acts had been the prohibition of this nonsense about gospels and charity and good works, — about translating the Scriptures, and assemblies of the people to be addressed by laymen. "No Houses of Bread nor Houses of God, except such as the Chapter builds!" And one of his first victories was that which he won over Pierre Waldo when he excommunicated him and his, and when the Pope confirmed the excommunication. For, only six years before, just as Fine-House was buying his fief, Pope Alexander had embraced this barefoot beggar, and had approved his life of voluntary poverty.

But it was one thing to drive the merchant-preacher and his friends out of Lyons, and another to make the people forget them. There were too many who had been fed by their bounty, comforted by their sympathy, and taught by their zeal, who were too insignificant for exile, but were too grateful to forget. The weaver Prinhac was one of these; and by the secret signals which they had established among themselves, he knew that many of the men-at-arms of the Chapter thought as he thought and felt as he felt. It was his confidence in their help which had brought him out over the bridge so easily.

But in truth Jean Waldo had chosen him only because he had seen that he was quick as a flash and faltered at nothing. It had been, alas, not from any deep religious feeling, but from the agony of despair, that Jean Waldo had summoned the young athlete to rise, "for the love of Christ." The man had replied to the summons so fortunately made, with the reply which, to one initiated into the mysteries of these "poor men," would have shown that he was one who was loyally tied to the teachers and friends who had done so much for Lyons, and were exiled from their homes. But Jean Waldo was not initiated, and he had no suspicion that he had made a choice so happy as he had when he sent Prinhac upon his errand.

Prinhac and Barbe-Noire crossed the causeway more slowly than either of them liked, but as fast as the rider dared to go over an icy road in the darkness. As day began to break at last, they came to a point for which Giulio's directions had not prepared him. He had crossed the river again. The valley road, which in our time is the road always travelled, was but a half-broken way, little better than a foot-path. The beaten track turned to the left and boldly pushed up the steep hill. The foot-path was stolen from the edge of the hill, which here crowds close upon the Rhone. Still, though it was narrow, and though, clearly enough, a block of ice from the river or of rock from the cliff might easily make it impassable, it was so much more level and so much more direct than the hill road, that Prinhac would have been glad to choose it. But he did not dare, without better authority than his own guess or wish.

A miserable turf hovel stood some hundred yards back from the way he had been following, on a steep slope of the hill. Unwilling to lose an instant, the young man still forced Barbe-Noire, who seemed as unwilling as himself, across the little turnip-patch, and bringing the horse close to the very door itself, knocked loud enough to waken Ogier the Dane.

No answer.

Prinhac knocked again and again. It was no deserted hovel, he knew that; and he meant that no one there should sleep later that morning.

To the fourth knock, the squeaking voice of an old woman answered: "Who is there?"

"O," said the rider, laughing, "you have turned over in the bed, have you? I am a courier from Lyons, and I want to know which is my best way to Meximieux."

"Both are the best — both are the best. Go your way, and do not be waking honest people at midnight!"

Prinhac had played on a word in calling himself a courier. A courier was indeed a carrier of messages, and it was true that he was carrying a message: but in the phrase of the time, a "courier" in Lyons corresponded to what we now call a prosecuting attorney, and Prinhac had had the hope that he might frighten the old crone into an answer. But he reckoned quite without his host. The truth was, that she did not know the word in either of its meanings. She only guessed that here was some roysterer who was to be kept at bay, and answered as best she could, with the object of getting rid of him.

Prinhac waited a moment, but found he was to get no other answer. He knocked again and again, but there was no answer. It was half unconsciously that he said then, in no loud tone, "For the love of Christ, will no one show me the way?"

And the answer was as prompt as his own had been to Jean Waldo. The shutter of the hovel was thrown open wide. A man thrust half his body out from the window.

"Who pleads the love of Christ? If you have all day before you, take the valley; but you take the chances of having to return. If your errand is haste, take the hill road. Trust me, for I speak it

IN HIS NAME."

The rider nodded, made the Cross of Malta in the air, pushed his horse down to the roadway again, and began the tedious ascent of the hill.

As he rose from the fog of the valley, he turned uneasily in his saddle and looked back once and again to be sure what was the prospect of the weather now sunrise drew near. For if this day were to be stormy, if the hill paths were to be blocked or obscured by never so little freshly-fallen snow, little hope was there that the priest-doctor for whom he was sent would ever see little Félicie alive. Prinhac was of a hopeful mood. But he found it hard to read the signs of the times in that early morning, hard indeed to persuade himself that the rifted clouds which were beginning to catch their glory of purple and gold from the sun still concealed, were only to be painted clouds that day, and that there was no malice behind them. "The mountain will tell me," said Prinhac. "If, when I have passed the castle gate, I see the white mountain, I will lay a wager on the day; but if there are as heavy clouds before me as there are behind, it must go hard with poor Mademoiselle Félicie."

And they toiled up the broken hill, Prinhac and the horse. Prinhac was not too lazy nor too proud to save his horse, even at this early hour, as best he might. At the heaviest ascent, he was off the saddle and walked by the noble creature's side, only playing with the thick and heavy black mane, which had given to him his name. Then, without waiting for stirrups, he was on his back again, and he indulged Barbe-Noire in a little gallop as they crossed the flat which is commanded by the castle.

The heavy square tower of the castle seemed completely to block the way. But Prinhac advanced, nothing faltering, — rode close along the wall, turned it, and opened on a vision of wonder such as he never looked upon before.

The hill which he had been mounting commands from its highest ridge a marvellous view of the valley of the Rhone. Far beneath him lay the winding course of the river, flowing between fields which were this morning white with hoar-frost. The blue of the Rhone and the white of the frost both revealed themselves to him through the exquisite purple mist which even at this hour was beginning to rise from the meadows. Like islands through this mist, Prinhac could see one and another village, — here a tower, and there a square castle, — he could see the spires of Lhuis and St. Laurent, and far away Arandon. But he did not pause to look or to wonder. He pressed his horse to the point where the prospect opens most to the eastward, and there, against the purple and the gold of the sunrise, — the sun himself not having struggled yet above the mountains, — there he saw the monarch of them all, lying purple-gray against this blazing background, without one fillet of cloud across his face, nor a wreath of mist rising from his valleys.

The weaver accepted the signal he had been longing for. "Ah, Monsieur Mont Blanc!" he said aloud, "you are a good friend to my Mistress Félicie this day."

How little the good fellow thought that as lately as sunset on the evening before, his young "mistress" had been throwing her kisses from the hill of Fourvières over to her "dear old friend."

And now he and Barbe-Noire were fairly in for their work. More than two hours had passed since he crept out of Lyons in the darkness, and daylight must make up for the time which had been lost in the creeping. Barbe-Noire was as glad as he for the right to take a quicker pace, — and now began the real triumph of blood and good temper and good breeding. It was not long that the road held the high ground. As the sun at last rose glorious behind the Alps themselves and the thousand ranges of castellated mountains which lay against the heavy line of the Alps, the descent into the valley again began. The rider looked his last on Félicie's old friend, and let his faithful horse take as fast a pace as he dared in the descent. Once on the flats again, their pace was like flying. The country children on their way to morning mass looked with wonder, and indeed with terror, as they saw this coal-black horse, with nostrils open and eyes of fire, dash by them. The rider was no knight, they could see that. But not even when the knights from Burgundy came through to join in the crusade had these children seen such a horse or such a rider. So Prinhac passed village after village, group after group of church-goers, and began to feel that his work was more certain of success than he had feared, and that he should find the hidden doctor, as he must find him, before noon of that day. If only back in the hills there were any horse to bring the doctor back who could compare with this brave Barbe-Noire!

Ah, Prinhac! ah, Prinhac! What says the Scripture? "The race is not to the swift nor the battle to the strong." As he was passing through the little hamlet of Dagnieu, nodding good-naturedly to a group of frightened children, who were huddling together by the hedge that they might be out of his way, Barbe-Noire trod with his forefoot on a sheet of ice, disguised under a cloud of slime which had flowed down on it the day before. The horse slipped, tried to rally, and lost the regularity of his pace; slipped again, brought up his hind feet on the same treacherous ice, and before his master could draw foot from stirrup, horse and rider had fallen heavily upon the stones of the wayside.

Prinhac uttered no sound. But he was fettered for the moment beneath the weight of the horse and was powerless. Poor Barbe-Noire did his best — his very best. Is the poor fellow maimed? That was Prinhac's first thought, — whether he himself were maimed would appear afterwards.

Then he made outcry enough to call to his aid, first a frightened girl, and then her brothers, and then every man and woman of the wretched hamlet. Barbe-Noire had in the mean while struggled to his feet. But Barbe-Noire would never bear rider again. In that cruel fall the horse's slender fore-leg had broken just above the fetlock; and though Prinhac and the rest tried to persuade themselves that this was but a sprain, every effort the poor beast made was more painful to see, and it needed only the most tender touch at the place where the bone was broken, to know that the calamity could never be cured.

For poor Prinhac himself the fall had been as hard. "I would not say a word," he said, "if the horse could only move." But whether he chose to say a word or no, none the less was it clear that his left shoulder on which he had fallen was powerless. The truth was, that his arm had been wrenched from its socket by the blow.

The peasants were stupid, but were kind. One and all they offered such help as they could, and suggested this and that cabin as open to Prinhac till the priest could be sent for; or at Balan below there was a famous farrier. If the gentleman wished, Odo, here, should be sent on the gray mare for him. But Prinhac listened with little favor to any talk of the priest, nor did he seem to care much for the farrier. "This is what I want, my brave friends," he said. "I want to send a bit of vellum as big as your two fingers to the doctor who is in the hills beyond Rambert de Joux. It is not three hours' ride. Who will go there?"

Stupidly they all listened, and no one answered. There was a look of inquiry which passed from each to each which would have been droll were not the occasion so serious. It seemed to say: "Is the man a simpleton, or does he think we are simpletons?"

"Fifty sols in silver," said Prinhac, cheerfully, "to the man who will take this bit of paper to the charcoal-burner Mark of Seyssel. Who is the man, or who is the pretty girl that will do it?" as his eye fell on a sunburned maiden. "Fifty sols to a man, or sixty to a girl."

But they stood as if he spoke Hebrew to them, and neither girl nor man replied.

"Is there nobody," said Prinhac, discouraged more by his failure than his pain,—"nobody who is willing to save a dying woman's life for the love of Christ?"

"You should have asked that before!" said a tall, lithe man, speaking in the purest Romance. He had seemed perfectly indifferent, even unconscious, until he heard these last words. "You should have asked that before. Antoine, Marie, take these brats home. Paul, Jean, Pierre, the whole troop of you, lead this poor beast to the priest's house, and groom him well. Felix, show the gentleman the way to Our Lady's stile. Then he turned to Prinhac,—

"This is a noble horse, my friend, who has borne you well; but the Arab who is to take me to your doctor, can give minutes to any beast in the Abbot's stables, and shall still win the crown. You will find me at Our Lady's stile, ready to serve you,—

'In His Name.'"

Sure enough, when poor Prinhac, who walked stoutly and stiffly, leaning his whole weight, as it seemed, on the shoulder of this willing Felix,—when he came to Our Lady's stile, here was his new friend mounted on a noble Arab, of the breed which at that time was just finding its way into Southern France from the ports of the southern shore. Prinhac took from his pocket the precious missive, and whispered to the workman the directions he had received from Giulio the Florentine. The villager had a little switch in his hand with which he marked in the air the sign of the Cross of Malta. The poor, faint weaver did the same with his finger; and they parted, the one for his quick ride, the other for such comfort as he could find in the cabin of Pierre Boronne.

CHAPTER V.

LOST AND FOUND.

Gualtier of the Mill knew every inch of the way before him, knew where and how to spare his horse, where to take a short cut by ways known to scarcely any except the charcoal-burners, where to ford a stream, and how to save a hill. So far he had the advantage for this service of poor Prinhac, whose zeal had cost him so dearly. And Gualtier of the Mill trusted more openly to the talisman which they had both been using. As he worked his way into the mountains, he had less fear of any spies or tip-staves of the Bishop and his crew, and did not hesitate to show the flag under which he served. It happened to him, as it happened to Prinhac, to come upon one of the draw-bridges which so often held the roadway where it crossed a stream. But the moment Gualtier appeared on the height above, it was enough for him to mark in the air with the sign of the Cross of Malta, and the attendants of the bridge, some sort of rural gens-d'armes known in those days, ran to let it down for the rider, who acknowledged the courtesy as he passed, by saying, gently, "It is for the love of Christ," and received, as he knew he should, the countersign, "And IN HIS NAME." The road became more and more hilly, but in an hour he had made more than three good leagues, and he came upon the picturesque height of Meximieux just as the people from village and from castle had poured into the church for the Sunday service of the day.

Gualtier looked round him and saw no man. He rode to the church door, swung himself from the horse, which he left wholly unfastened, and entered in the midst of the assembly, who were upon their knees. Gualtier knelt also, and joined in the devotions; but at the first change in the order of the service, he noted one worshipper whose white head was still hidden in his hands, bent over him, and whispered "For the Love of Christ." The old man rose without a word, and they left the church together. A moment's conference, and he bade Gualtier wait for him where the road turns from the stable-gate of the castle, he swung himself over the hedge-stile and was gone. Gualtier of the Mill walked his horse to the fork in the road which had been indicated, and at the same moment the gray-haired villager was there with the best horse from the Baron's stable. Gualtier left his own in his care, saluted as before, and was gone. "It is IN HIS NAME," said his new-found friend.

Two hours from Meximieux with riding so fast should have brought him to the charcoal-burner's hut, which had been indicated all along as the station at which he was aiming. But these were no longer ways for travellers. They were only the paths that fagot-makers or charcoal-burners had made for their convenience between rocks, bushes, and trees, and which at their convenience they neglected again. Gualtier of the Mill used his sense as long as any man's sense could save him at all. He chose such paths as led a little south of east, as he had been bidden. He got a glimpse now and then of the stronghold above Rossillon, passed, as he was bidden, the castle of Vieux-Mont-Ferrand; but at last, in a tangle of low, scrubby oaks, and amid piles of rocks which seemed to have been hurled together in some play of ogres, no path looked promising among the sheep-tracks and the traces of the feet of the asses and mules, from whose charcoal loads the litter still strewed the ground.

Gualtier of the Mill stopped, fairly confounded. He blew a shrill whistle, and had no answer. He dropped his reins on the neck of his horse, and his horse stood still He faithfully tried the pathway which seemed to trend most to the eastward, and it led him in fifty yards distance to the place where chips on the ground showed that the wood-cutters had taken out some saplings there, and had gone no farther. He came back to the "abomination of desolation," as it seemed to him, sat undecided, though he knew indecision was ruin, and it seemed to him a voice from heaven when he heard the loud laugh of a little child.

In an instant the child was hushed, and all was still again. But the sound was enough for Gualtier of the Mill. He pushed his horse to the place it came from, through a close thicket of tangled cedars which he had refused to try before, and after a steep descent came out on a group of a dozen frightened children by the side of a brook. They had been at play there, had heard his horse's footsteps, and had been frightened into silence by the sound. For in the lawlessness of those times, the havoc made by everybody who rode on horseback, whether he rated himself as knight, squire, man-at-arms, or highwayman, was such that peasant children like these, in such a wilderness as this, had much the same notion of such travellers as had the old crone whom Prinhac had summoned in the early morning. And so the older brothers and sisters of this group had been trying to keep the little ones silent till the horseman should go by.

Gualtier of the Mill drew up his horse when he saw the pretty company, and in a cheerful way said, "Who is playing fox and goose here?" And the little children hid behind the bigger ones, and the bigger ones hung their heads, and said nothing.

"And which of you can tell me the way to the house of Mark of Seyssel, where the road from Culoz comes in?"

The little children hid behind the bigger ones, and the bigger ones hung their heads, as before.

"Now I really hoped," said the good-natured miller, "I really hoped I had found one of Mark's little girls; and I really hoped she would show me the way. At my home I have four girls and five boys, and they all know all the sheep-tracks and all the horse-tracks. And when Father Antony comes and says, 'Who will mount my mule and show me the way?' why Jean runs, and Gertrude runs, and Antoine runs, and Marie runs, and all of them want to show him."

The miller understood the way to children's hearts. But these children had been trained to hold their peace among strangers. More than once, as the older of them knew, had life depended on their discretion; and so stolid were their faces as Gualtier of the Mill tried his seductions, that even he was deceived. He fairly thought they did not know what the words meant which he was speaking.

He drew from his pocket the silver whistle which he had blown just before. He sprang from his horse, and let the creature go at large. He sat down on the ground by the youngest child, and with the whistle, which was a flageolet indeed, of the range of a few notes, played, for the child's amusement, a little air; and then taking the little thing upon his knee, tried if he would not take the plaything. The child seemed to dread the reproof of the older children, but the bauble was too tempting to be resisted; and when the pipe gave out a shrill, sharp sound at his effort, the little thing laughed and became more fearless, and seemed more willing to be won. Gualtier followed up his victory; and in the rough dialect of the Dauphin Mountains, which he spoke as easily as the Provençal in which he had been talking, he said again, —

"It is Mark of Seyssel, the charcoal merchant, whom I want to find. Mark of Seyssel has some good little girls. Do you not know his little girls? I have a bright silver sol here for each of them."

You are a cunning fowler, Gualtier, and you are a keen fisherman. But here are fish who will not bite at every bait. It is one of Mark's little boys whom you have upon your knee. And that tall, brave child, whose hair is braided in with a strip of red ribbon, is one of his girls. But they know too well that they are to say nothing of roads unless they know they speak to friends. And not a flash of intelligence passes from one heavy eye to another.

Then the miller wondered if perhaps these oldest children, wise as he saw them to be, had been trusted with secrets more precious than the mere guarding of a roadway. Still speaking in the mountain dialect, he said, as if he were speaking to the wind, without addressing one child more than another, "This is life and death for which I am travelling. A dear, loving girl will die this night, if, before the sun is at noon, I do not find the house of Mark of Seyssel. I wonder if any one could show me his house if I asked for the Love of Christ?"

The brown-haired girl, and the stupid boy, and the other boy who held the long, peeled rod, and the other tall girl who had a baby in her arms — all started at the spell. The first of the four spoke in Provençal, and said, "I will lead you gladly to my father's, now I know you come

In His Name."

And in a minute more he was in the saddle again; the child was sitting across it before him, he was pushing through this tangle and over that ford, scrambling up a hill-side, and then threading a low growth of under brush, till in less than a mile from the point where he had lost himself, the girl found voice again; and, speaking in Provençal as before, said, "There is my father's storehouse." And as she pointed, on the other side of a little clearing in the forest, he saw a rough cabin, built half of logs and half of rough stones. From a hole in the roof, quite too large, and indeed of too little architectural form, to be called a chimney, a volume of smoke was pouring. Without this token, indeed, the loud voices of the men within would have taught the traveller that the charcoal-burner's hut was not deserted.

CHAPTER VI.

THE CHARCOAL-BURNER.

The science of the iron forges in the valley below had already reached some work so fine that the workmen there had instructed the peasants of the hills, and sent them to a separate industry of burning and packing pine, chestnut, and oak charcoal, to be used in the manufacture of the finer steels. Many a man who was part hunter and part shepherd was willing to provide himself with his salt, with a few nails, with iron heads to his arrows, and with better pipkins and mugs than they baked in the mountains, by answering the demand. The rough fellows had found, however, that it was better to make but one business of their trade with the iron and steel men; and so now, for a generation and more, this rough cabin, where Mark of Seyssel now presided, had become a rendezvous for the charcoal-burners, and they had been in the habit of storing here the full bags in which they had packed their coals ready for the mules.

In the middle of the cabin or hut, on an open place for fire, there were piled a dozen great logs, which made a cheerful point of union for the group, and from which, through a great, square hole in the roof, passed out the weird column of smoke which first caught the eye of the traveller. Around this, sitting and lying in every possible attitude, was the company of the lazy peasants, getting rid of the winter day as best they could.

"If you ever see Lambert this side of purgatory, call me a liar. When I saw him cross the old bay, with his new baldric on him, I said, 'Good-by, Lambert, we shall never meet again.' And I said it because I knew it."

"But why do you know it, and how do you know it?" persisted the man with whom the speaker was talking. He sat shaping a bow, and letting the shavings of ash fall upon the live coals, as he made them. "How do you know it? Here at Blon I talked with the innkeeper, with all the grooms, and with Sirand himself. They all said that the Saracens would not stand the first battle with our men. They said there would be a new king at Jerusalem before Easter; and that long before another Christmas the Bishop would be at Lyons again, King Philip in Paris, King Richard in England; and by the same token the count will be in his castle, and Lambert and Raymond and Forney and all the boys would be back here, with shells on their hats, and with gold in their pockets."

"Much does Sirand know," retorted the implacable grumbler, who began: "Has he talked with the Saracens? Has their famous king, the Lord Saladin, told him that they were all going to run away at the first battle? Has he been to see Jerusalem, that he thinks it a summer day's journey to go there? As for the innkeeper at Blon, the man is a fool. The last time I was there, he would have persuaded me to my face that I did not know a walnut bow from one made of ash. I wish he may be choked with his own porridge. And if his grooms know no more of Saladin's men than they know of Frenchmen's horses, their talk is not worth retailing. I tell you it is a fool's errand they have all gone upon, and you will never see Lambert's face again."

"Is it a fool's errand," struck in a little, lame man who sat on the other side of the fire, so that the two could hardly see him, "to redeem the grave of our blessed Lord, and our blessed Lady, his mother, and of more saints than I could name or you can count, from these misbegotten dogs, heathen and sons of heathen? Did you hear the father tell how they flayed alive that poor Mary of Picardy when she went on a pilgrimage? Did you hear him tell how they built their cursed fire against St. Joseph's tomb, and cracked the columns, and heaved dirt upon the stone? Fool's errand indeed! It's well for them to call it a fool's errand who stay idling here at home. But had I two feet to walk, or a leg to cross a mule, I would not be hanging round here, throwing shame on better men."

"Limping Pierre," replied the other, good-naturedly, "I have heard you say that thing before, or what came to the same end; and, if you choose, you may say it seven times more, nay, seventy times seven, as the gospel says, and I will never quarrel with as good a fellow as you are. But two things you know and I know: one is, that Ambrose cared no more for our Lady nor for St. Joseph's tomb than he cared for the snow on the top of the mountain, nor would he go one step of his lazy life to save them both from pollution. He went because he saw the others go, and he chose to be fed without working, and to sleep on linen that other men's wives had woven. He thought he should come back with gold he had not earned, and should hector over you and me and other honest people because he had a shell in his hat-band. As for making war upon people because they are dogs and the sons of dogs, because their prayers are false, and their lives mean, — why we might make war on the Bishop and Chapter of Lyons for quite as good cause as they have to make war on King Saladin and his Emirs, if that happens to be his name."

The bold effrontery of the allusion to the bishop and chapter was welcomed by a guffaw of laughter from some of the lazy throng; but others fairly started, not so much in anger as in terror. "Keep a civil tongue in your head, Matthew, or it will be the worse for all of us. There is treason enough and heresy enough talked in this store to give all the hamlets over to the Couriers, and we may be sent a-begging before we know it with our wives and our children."

But to this protest Mark of Seyssel himself made answer, speaking for the first time: —

"Jean Fisherman, if you do not like the talk here, you need not stay here. If you have any gossip to retail to the Courier or the Viguier you had better go and retail it, and good riddance to you. I am master of this hovel, and it is my castle; when I am afraid of my guests, I will turn them out-doors. Till I am afraid of them, they will not check each other's talk. For my own part," said the burly collier, "I am quite of black-eyed Matt's mind, and I drink his very good health. When the pot is white, it may scold the kettle for being black; but while the priests and the abbots send men from their homes because they feed the poor, when they take their houses and steal their goods to make themselves comfortable, why, if they do go to the Holy Land with his Grace the King and his Holiness the Bishop, I am afraid they will carry no better Gospel than they left behind. For my part I wish I could see men here live as the saints lived, before they go to whip the Saracens into living so." And the stout collier took from the settle by him a tankard from which he had been drinking, passed it to black-eyed Matthew, as he called the bow-maker, and bade him give to the others to drink in their turn.

It was just as he had done this, that there was heard at the heavy doorway the sharp rap of the handle of Gualtier's riding-whip, and on the instant the charcoal-burner bade him enter. The man seemed a little surprised at the sight of his own daughter with the stranger. The child clearly felt that her duty was done. She dropped a courtesy, and was off to the shelter of the shrubbery in an instant.

The collier offered Gualtier a seat by the fire. But the whole assembly was hushed, so that no one would have guessed that they were all in talk so eager only the moment before.

"Are you Mark the collier?" said the messenger. "I am told that you can direct me to the house of Father Jean of Lugio."

"Eh?" was the only reply of the stout collier, who but just now was so voluble, and was defending so volubly the sacred rights of volubility in others.

"I have been riding, at my best, to find Father Jean of Lugio. I am told he makes his home in these parts. And he is needed, sorely needed, to-day in Lyons. I have a message for him here."

"Eh?" was the grunt again, which the fuller explanation extorted from the collier. Gualtier was surprised. He had never seen this man, but he had not supposed him to be an idiot. And he had certainly supposed that a person who transacted so much business in the valley would have some knowledge of the Provençal. But he repeated his explanation, and more at length, in the hill dialect, in which he had spoken to the collier's children.

"Eh?" was the stupid reply as before. But then the clown looked up heavily upon the others, and in the same language said, "Boys, do you hear what the gentleman says? Do any of you know anything of this Jean of Lugio, this father whom he has come to see?"

The men looked stupidly upon each other, as if they could not understand this dialect any more than he could understand the Provençal of the miller.

Gualtier looked round to see if one face were any more intelligent than the others. Then he took from his pocket six or eight pieces of silver, tossed them in the air, and caught them again in his hand. Speaking in the same dialect he said, "These are for any good fellow who will go to the house of the father for me; and here are as many more for any one who comes back with him." But a dead, stupid wonder, which hardly counted for curiosity, was the only emotion which seemed to be aroused, even by this unwonted display. Gualtier of the Mill felt as if, even at the last moment, he was foiled. "A tall man," he said, "with a tonsure, and the hair around it, as white as snow. He bends a little as he walks, he is so tall; he favors his right foot in walking."

"Eh?" from Mark of Seyssel, was the only answer.

Gualtier was provoked with himself that he had not kept the child. The child at least could speak, and could understand. It seemed to him that of the group of idlers there was not one, no, not the stout head of the castle himself, who seemed to take the least interest in his mission. Far less could they help him, if they had chosen.

Provoked with himself for letting the child go, he walked again to the door to see if he could trace her; but she was out of sight long ago. He turned back, and the others were sitting as stolidly as he found them. On the instant, however, the inspiration came to him, and he saw that the talisman by which he had succeeded with her might be as effective with these churls. In truth, the dulness of the men had entirely deceived him. He had lost his presence of mind, and was fairly confused by the charcoal-dealer's well-acted stupidity. As Gualtier closed the door again, he took up a bit of charcoal from the floor, and, as if to amuse himself in a careless habit, on the door itself drew roughly a Roman cross, of which the vertical line was not longer than the cross bar, and then with a few touches improved upon it till it became the Cross of Malta, with its sharp points and re-entering angles at each extremity.

Beneath the cross he wrote in Latin the two words, "Amore Christi."

Before he had finished the inscription, the bow-maker had risen from the ground and was putting on his outer jerkin, as if to leave the fire. Two others of the idlers, also, seemed to have done all they had to do in the cabin, and made as if they were going away. Mark of Seyssel himself said aloud, "It's nigh to noon, and I shall sit here no longer. If François, comes bid him ask the old woman where I am." So saying he brushed out by Gualtier, and as he opened the door, said to him, "Come away from them into the air." As the miller followed him, he led the way apart from ear-shot in the house, and said, "You should have made some signal before. There are men in that hut that would gladly put the Father in irons, and throw him into the lake of Bourget. But you can trust me, and indeed more than me, if you come

In His Name."

Then Gualtier told the awakened savage who he was, and why he came; that he had in his hand what he was told it was of the first importance that the Father should know that he had been bid to bring this missive:— "For the love of Christ," and that he had agreed to do so, "IN HIS NAME." He told Mark of Seyssel that as token of his truth, he would trust the parchment to him, and that he might carry it to the master's hiding-place; that the master then could make his own choice whether to come or to refuse. "Only this I know, said the miller, "that if he do not show himself at this spot ready to mount my horse here when the sun is at noon, I see no use of his coming here at all; for the order is that he is to cross the bridge at Lyons before the sun goes down. You know, my friend," said he, "that he is a brave horseman who makes that distance in that time."

The collier hurried away. The rider returned into the hut and threw himself on the ground by Jean the fisherman. Jean was anxious enough to try to find out who the stranger was, and to learn more of the errand on which he had come; but Gualtier was as shrewd as he was, parried question with question, and for an hour the group was as much in doubt as when he found them as to his business. He had sense enough to produce a flask of wine from behind the saddle of his horse, and offered this in token of good-fellowship to the company. They talked about the frost, about the freshet, about the price of coal, about the new mines of iron; and they had approached the central subject of the great crusade again, when Mark of Seyssel again entered the smoky cabin.

He took the place he had left by the fire, and said to the miller, "I have given to your horse all the oats I had, and he has eaten them all."

He said this gruffly; and those who were not in the secret might well imagine, as he meant they should, that his interview with the stranger had related chiefly to his horse's welfare. Gualtier thanked him with the good nature he had shown all along, counted out copper enough to pay for the oats, bade the party good-by, and said he would go farther on his journey. He crossed the opening to the place where the horse was tethered, and there und r the juniper-tree to which he was fastened, he found, as he had hoped to find, Father Jean of Lugio.

CHAPTER VII.

JOHN OF LUGIO.

JOHN OF LUGIO is one of the men who did the world service wellnigh inestimable in his day, and who is to-day by the world at large, forgotten. When one reads in the Epistle to the Hebrews of men who had trial of mockings and scourgings, of bonds and imprisonments; who were destitute, afflicted, tormented; who wandered in deserts and mountains and dens and caves of the earth, — "of whom the world was not worthy,"— one ought to remember for a moment that he owes it to a few groups of just such men, one of whom was this forgotten John of Lugio, that he is able to read those words at all, or is indeed permitted to do so.

When Peter Waldo, the prosperous merchant of Lyons, was first awakened to the value of the gospel for all men around him, and saw their ignorance of it as well, he gave himself and his means not only to feeding the hungry and finding homes for the homeless, but to wayside instruction in the words of Christ. He found one and another version of parts of the Old and New Testament in the Romance language. The very oldest specimen of that language which we have to-day is a paraphrase, of a generation or two before Peter Waldo's time, of the Bible history. It is known by the name of the "Noble Lesson." The troubadours, whom we are wont to think of as mere singers of love songs and romances, were in those days quite as apt to sing these sacred songs, and they carried from place to place a more distinct knowledge of the Bible stories than the people gained in churches.

Peter Waldo undertook to improve the popular knowledge of the Bible thus gained. This was an important part of his enterprise. He had himself a sufficient knowledge of Latin to read the Latin Vulgate. To translate this into the language of Provence, he gained the assistance of three intelligent priests, all of them in office in Lyons. They were Bernard of Ydros, Stephen of Empsa, and John of Lugio, with whom the reader is now to become acquainted. Neither of the three supposed that there was anything exceptional in their enterprise, as how should they? They and their friend were at work to teach the common people the "Word of God" more simply and perfectly, and what better could they do? Of the three, Stephen undertook the work of translation especially; John examined the other translations and compared them with Stephen's,— he studied the critics, sought in every direction the best authorities, and made this new Bible of the people as perfect as careful scholarship and the best learning of the time could do. Bernard took the more humble part of transcribing the text agreed upon,—more humble but not less important. Probably a careful explorer in the old convent libraries of the South of France might now find his patient manuscripts, even after the ruthless destruction wrought by the persecutors of that century and the century which followed. When Peter Waldo made his journey to Rome, to ask for the benediction of the Pope on their labors, one or all of these men probably accompanied him. As has been said already, the Pope was only too glad to find that such assistance in the organization of religion was raised up among the laymen of Lyons. The scheme prepared was very much like that which St. Francis proposed only a few years later; where it differed from his, it differed in a more broad and generous understanding of the needs of the great body of the people.

If only the bishop and chapter of Lyons had been equal to the exigency! But, alas, they were not equal to it. To them the great reality of religion was their newly-bought temporal power over the city and country. The interference of merchants, whether as almoners or as lay readers in the affairs of the city, was no part of their plan. They had not bought out the Count of Forez, and freed themselves from his dictation, to be dictated to now by a set of fanatics within their own wall. They therefore, as has been said, refused all approval to the far-seeing plans of Peter Waldo; they excommunicated him and his, confiscated their property, and drove them from their homes.

Such crises try men's souls, and it is from such fires that tempered metal only comes out uninjured. Of the four men who had worked together in the distribution of the new Bible, two were taken and two were left. Peter Waldo endured the loss of all things, travelled over the world of Europe, and left everywhere his great idea of a Bible for the people, and of a church in which layman as well as priest was a minister to God. Bernard and Stephen could not stand the test. They made their peace with the authorities of the Lyonese church, and no man knows their after history. John of Lugio, whom we ask the reader of these lines to remember among the men of whom the world of his own time was not worthy, never turned back from the plough. He had consecrated his life to this idea of a free Bible. To this idea he gave his life. It would be hard to name any city of Central Europe, even as far as Bohemia, which did not profit by his counsels and his studies. And when John Huss went to the stake, in loyalty to the same idea, he and the men around him were willing to acknowledge their obligation to John of Lugio and to Peter Waldo.

The priest stood waiting for the miller, curious to know what manner of man he was who had so resolutely brought the message which he held. He was not himself dressed in the costume of any ecclesiastical order. Nor was he, on the other hand, dressed as any nobleman, far less as any soldier of the time would have been. He might have been taken for some merchant's messenger, sent back from Lyons into the country on a message about flax or woollen. His white hair appeared below a traveller's hat; his tonsure of course was invisible. His surcoat was tightly buttoned, as for a cold ride. There was nothing in the color or in the fashion of his costume such as would challenge the remark of any wayfarer.

"I am not Jean Waldo's own messenger," was the immediate reply of Gualtier of the Mill, to his first inquiry; "I am only, as you see, a 'Poor Man of Lyons,' who was recognized as such by our secret password when the messenger to whom Jean Waldo gave this mission fell with his good horse almost at my house door. It was clear enough that if the message meant anything it meant speed. This Prinhac crossed the draw-bridge at Lyons before daybreak, because the bridge was held by one of our people; but one cannot tell if there shall be any such good fortune this evening. The bridge may be held by your worst enemy. Why! you have scant five hours to make these twelve leagues which have cost us wellnigh seven hours. True, you have to go down the hills, which we have had to climb. Your horses will be ready, while ours had to be groomed and saddled. But, holy father, it will not answer to have any horse fall under you; for, if I understand the message I have brought, it is not every lay-brother who can take your place to-night at yon girl's bedside."

Father John would not even smile. "The Lord will direct," he said, "and the Lord will provide. Whether my journey helps or hinders, only the Lord knows. But it seems to be His work. For the love of Christ I am summoned, and IN HIS NAME I go. Young man," he added, as Gualtier of the Mill adjusted for him the stirrups of the noble horse who was to bear him, "when I left Lyons, they burned in the public square the precious books to which I had given twenty of the best years of this little life. What I could do for God and his Holy Church, they vainly tried to destroy. They compelled me to part from my own poor; from the widows whose tears were sacred; from the orphans I had taught and had fed; from humble homes, which are as so many temples to me of God's well-beloved Son. I said then, as their mocking Viguier led me to the draw-bridge, which I am to pass to-night, and bade me 'Begone,'—I said, I will not see you henceforth till the day in which ye shall say, 'Blessed is he that cometh in the name of the Lord.' Young man, this Jean Waldo to whose household I am bidden lifted no hand for me that day, nor for his kinsman, my noble friend, nor for one of the Poor Men of Lyons, or her Poor Women or Children. But time brings its recompense; and to-day he is praying God that I may come in time. Father Almighty, hear and answer his prayer; and grant thy servant wisdom and strength to render some service this day somewhere to thy children."

The Miller reverently said "Amen." The priest made the sign of the cross, and blessed him in parting, and then was gone.

That is a curious experience in which a man of fifty-five enters on an enterprise such as he has not tested for thirty years. He feels as young as ever, if he be a man of pure life. The spirit of man never grows old; it seems, indeed, to grow young, when it becomes as a little child every day. But John of Lugio knew that, when he was five-and-twenty, he would not have put his foot into the stirrup to spring into the saddle. He knew that he would not for such a day's adventure have girt on the surcoat he was wearing. "It is as well," he said to the spirited horse who bore him, "it is as well that you are not thirty years older than the gray stallion who bore me the last day I ever saw the great Bernard." And the memory of that day of his youth, and of its contrast with to-day, pleased him and engaged him for more than one mile. And any leader of men who should have watched his skill in handling his horse, and making the most of every advantage in the way, would have chosen the white-haired priest as he would hardly have chosen any younger man for service like this which engaged him. As physical strength declines,— and it does decline after the physical man is forty-five years old,— still experience, tact, habit of hand and eye, are all improving in a man well-governed and self-poised. And John of Lugio had not yet reached that age when the declining curve of physical strength crosses the ascending curve of experience and skill. There was not among all the crusaders who at that moment were trying a winter in Palestine, or on the way thither, one knight or squire more fit for hardy, active service than was he.

An hour's quick riding brought him to St. Rambert, where the Brevon, scarcely more than a brook, joins the larger stream called the Albarine. It was even then a quaint old town, which is just what the traveller would call it now. Its name is a corruption of that of St. Raynebert, a son of the Duke Radbert, a martyr of five centuries before John of Lugio's time and day. Before his time there had been some worship of Jupiter on the hills above, and the name of the old god lingered in the title "Joux," which hung even to the saint's name. St. Rambert de Joux was the name by which everybody knew the village. The brook plunges and rages in a series of cascades down a narrow valley, and the rider took a pathway down, which seemed wholly familiar to him, which led him under the walls of the Benedictine abbey. As he passed the gate, two of the brethren, in the costume of the order, came out after their noonday refection, and in the narrow pathway could not but look upon the rider's face, as he on them. They recognized him in an instant.

"Whither so fast, Brother John?" This was their salutation.

It was impossible not to draw bridle. And the first welcome of the two, impelled perhaps by the very suddenness of their meeting, was so cordial, that one must have been more cynical by far than John of Lugio not to respond with warmth and kindness. "My brother Stephen, my brother Hugh, are you two here? I was thinking of the brethren, but I did not know that you were so near. Father Ambrose does not send to me to tell me the names of the new arrivals."

"Father Ambrose will never send you the names of new arrivals more. He lies behind the chapel yonder, and we shall lay his body in the grave to-morrow." This was the immediate answer; and then there was an instant's pause, as they all recognized the awkwardness of their position.

John of Lugio was excommunicate. Whether they might speak to him in friendship was almost a question. That they ought in strictness to denounce him, and report to their superiors his presence in a town from which he had been formally banished — of this there could be no question. But the two monks were men and were Christians before they were monks, and with Jean both of them were united by old ties. "Will you rest your horse — will you rest yourself?" said Stephen, bravely. "I will take him myself into the stable, and Hugh will be only too glad to find you a cold dinner in the refectory. Your horse has travelled far; he will not be the worse for grooming."

"He must travel farther before he is groomed — and I. But I shall travel the lighter, Stephen, for the kind words you speak; and you will sleep the easier that you have spoken them. Do you, too, do your work, and I will do mine; and we will let nothing that men can do or can say part us. No — I must not stop. I would not put you two in danger by accepting your service, if I could; but I must do what few men do in these degenerate days, and cross the long bridge at Lyons before the sun goes down. Take the blessings of a Poor Man of Lyons, of a heretic, excommunicate! God bless you, my brother — and you!"

"God bless you, John; God bless you!" said the two, as they made way for his horse.

"It is for the love of Christ that I am speeding," said he, tenderly; "pray in your prayers to-day for the Father's blessing on me 'IN HIS NAME.'"

And they parted. If the monks were startled by the adventure, and they were, none the less was John of Lugio startled by it. He was not afraid of them. He had seen too clearly that the voice of the Holy Spirit had spoken to both of them more loudly than any rule or interdict. He knew that both of them would confess the sin of concealing his presence; that both of them would loyally do the penances appointed. He knew as well that neither of them would betray him, while betrayal would endanger him; and that neither of them, in his heart of hearts, would ever be sorry for the silent service rendered to him that day.

The adventure set him upon other thought than sympathy with them. Had he gratified the wishes and passion of his youth, his home would have been at this hour within those walls. He would have been the senior of every man, except Stephen, in that fraternity. He knew them all,— yes, and he knew perfectly well that not one of them affected to be his equal in the scholarship and learning to which the abbey was devoted. Humanly speaking, on the Abbot Ambrose's death, he himself, John of Lugio, would have become his successor, the lord of this lovely estate, the director in these noble ministries, the first student in these happy cloisters, if — if he had only obeyed the wish of his heart thirty years ago, and given himself here to student life!

But instead of that, Jean of Lugio had given himself to the immediate help of the Poor Men of Lyons. He had turned away from the fascination of study, to make the weavers and dyers and boatmen of Lyons purer men and happier; to bring comfort and life into their homes, and to make simpler their children's path to heaven. He had done this with his eyes open. He had turned away from the Abbey of Cornillon, and had made himself God's minister in the hovels of Lyons. And of this the reward was, that this day he hazarded his life by going back to Lyons to render one service more, while he might have been waiting, as the senior in the fraternity, within those happy abbey walls, to render fit service at the Abbot Ambrose's grave.

If — and the picture of half a life came in upon that if. But to John of Lugio that picture brought no regrets. He had chosen as his God directed him. In calmness he had foreseen what in the heat of conflict he had seen, and what he now looked back upon. Foreseeing, — seeing or looking back, — it was the picture of duty bravely done. And Father Jean passed down from under the walls of the abbey without a sigh or a tear.

The road still follows the stream, and the valley is by no means straight. Its curves are picturesque enough, but they do not lead a traveller very directly. He passed along the face of Mount Charvet, left the village of Serrières on his left, and came, before he dared to hope, to the new Castle of Montferrand. By a sudden determination he rode abruptly to the castle gate; and finding no warden, called loudly to a little boy whom he saw within, and bade him summon either a porter or some officer of the baron's household.

The truth was, that as he tried the Baron of Meximieux's noble gray stallion on one and another pace in descending the steep slopes from St. Rambert, it became painfully clear that the horse had done his work for that day. The miller had pressed him, perhaps, harder than he meant or knew; and, whatever care he had taken, the good horse had made near ten leagues, with only the hour's rest which had been given him at the cabin of Mark of Seyssel. If the priest were to succeed in the task assigned to him, he must make better speed than in the last hour he had made. This certainty determined his bold appeal at the castle.

A summons so hearty roused all its inmates, and they appeared at one or another door or corridor with that curiosity which in all times draws out the inhabitants of a lonely country-house, when there is chance to look upon some unexpected face, no matter of what human being. The Baron of Montferrand himself made his appearance. He was not dressed as if for King Philip's court, or for the Emperor's. In truth, he had spent the morning in the occupation — not very lordly, as we count lords, but perfectly baronial in the customs of his time — of directing the servants, who flayed and cut to pieces a fat boar which they had brought in at the end of yesterday's hunting. From this occupation, in which he had himself personally assisted, the baron had been called to dinner; and he had dined without the slightest thought of revising or improving his toilet. Before dinner was fairly over, he had fallen asleep in the chair, not uncomfortable, in which he sat at the head of the table. He was roused from his nap by the hurrying of one and another servant, as it was announced that a stranger was at the gate. A stranger in those days of December was not a frequent intruder.

John of Lugio was already talking with porter and seneschal. He was not displeased to see the baron approach him. The old man came bareheaded, and without any outer garment, beyond what he had worn at table, to protect him from the cold The traveller knew him on the instant; had seen him more than once in one or another journey up or down this valley, and, indeed, in closer intimacies, in the ministry of more than thirty years. But the baron, not caring a great deal for priests, and not having a great deal to do with them, did not for an instant suspect that the hardy rider with whom he had to do wore a tonsure, or had more than once lifted the consecrated chalice before him at the mass. He saluted the stranger somewhat abruptly, but still courteously, and invited him to dismount and rest himself.

"I thank you for your courtesy, my Lord," was the reply. "But my errand requires haste, as you will see. I am bidden to Lyons this very night, and that on service which brooks no delay. I had hoped that this horse, which is from the stables at Meximieux, would take me thither, and there a fresh beast waits me; but I have already taken from him the best that he can give, and he will make slow work of the long reach that is left for me. This is why I have stopped here: to ask, not your hospitality, but your help. If I may leave this good horse, and if you have another which will take me down the valley, you shall have my hearty thanks, and the blessings of the home where they need me."

"You tell your story frankly," said the baron; and with a stiff oath he added, "if I gave horses to every vagabond from the troop of Meximieux, I should have few horses left to give." Without farewell or apology, he turned to go back to his dining-hall.

"Pardon me, my Lord," persisted Father John, without the slightest passion or haste in his voice. "I am no man of the Baron of Meximieux. I am no man's man. I am sent for on a work of mercy, because one Jean Waldo thinks that I can save his child's life. If I am to serve her, I must be in Lyons to-night. If I am there, the service will be yours, not mine."

"If I should give horses to every beggar who chooses to ride out of Lyons, I should have no horses to give," said the baron. Like many men of little invention, he had been so much pleased by the cadence of his first retort, that he could not but try its force again. But the repetition of the insult gave the father courage. A man truly resolved does not say the same thing twice. Most likely he does not speak twice at all.

"I am no beggar from Lyons, or no servant of the Lyons merchant. Lyons does not love me, nor is there any reason but what I tell why I should care to enter Lyons But if you had a daughter dying, my Lord Baron, and Jean Waldo could send her a physician, you would be glad to have him send, though you never saw his face, and though you do not love his craft or his city. Can you not do as you would be done by?"

He had perhaps gained his point, though the baron, with a stupid notion that he must maintain his dignity in the presence of his own servants, tried to do so by a certain delay, which would have exasperated a person of less experience and less balance than Father John.

"How am I to know," said the wavering Montferrand, "that you are the leech you say you are? What is your token? If I am to give a horse to every quack who rides between Amberieux and St. Rambert, I should have no horses left to give."

"I have no token, my Lord. A man who has spoken truth for forty years, going up and down this valley, needs no token that he does not lie" He took off his hat as he spoke, and showed the tonsure. "You have received Christ's body from this hand, my Lord. You know that these lips will not speak falsely to you." And then, watching his man carefully, and noticing a change come on his face at the mention of the Saviour, he added as if by intention, and almost in a whisper: "It is for the love of Christ that I ask the best horse in your stables."

"Saddle Chilperic! Saddle Chilperic! Why are you clowns gaping and sneezing there? Saddle Chilperic! I say, and take this gentleman's good horse where he can be cared for. Take my hand, father, take my hand. Gently — so — you are stiff from riding. Come into the hall and let the baroness have a word with you! Chilperic will not be ready for a minute, and you will at least drink a glass of wine! If it only shows that you do not bear malice, you will drink a glass of wine! We are rough fellows, we hill barons, and we speak when we do not think, Father. But, indeed, indeed, I would have been more ready had you summoned me

'In His Name.'"

And he crossed himself as he passed the threshold.

In those surroundings, in the company in which they were, the baron did not dare question the priest further, nor explain how he had been initiated into the secret fraternity by the password of which he had been adjured. Nor did he care to say much to explain the inconsistency of his brutal refusal of one moment, when it was compared with his ready tenderness at the next. Perhaps it is best for all of us that we do not have to reconcile such inconsistencies as often as we are conscious of them. Once more he pressed the priest to refresh himself with wine, and he called loudly on his wife to join in his rough welcome as he entered the hall.

The little woman came forward, bending somewhat with rheumatism more than age, but with freshness and quickness, and with all the courtesy and dignity of noble breeding. Whether the grooms and other servants, and the idlers in the court-yard, had guessed the secret of the baron's sudden change of purpose, or had failed to guess it, she, who had seen the whole from her open casement, understood it all in a flash. Now that Father John entered the room she recognized him in an instant, as the baron had not done. But she knew very well that his liberty and possibly even his life depended on his passing on his errand unrecognized by her servants, and her perfect manner, therefore, was exactly what it would have been had he been any other person — a friend of the Lyonese weaver — summoned in hot haste to his daughter's bedside She dropped her courtesy, advanced to take the hat of the traveller, begged him to sit at her husband's side at the head of the table, and with her own hand poured the wine from the coarse jug which held it, into the highly-wrought cup which the bustling baron had found for his guest. "I heard something said of a lady — a girl — a sick girl. Is there nothing I can send from our stores? I could in a moment put up maiden-wort, or rosemary, or St. Mary's herb, if your reverence will only take them."

But the Father thanked her and declined. His friends in Lyons must have at their command such drugs as could be of service, if anything can be of service indeed.

"Ah, sir," she said, "if only you will render service to them, like the blessing you once gave to me!"

"To you!" and he looked amazed into those sharp little black eyes, which twinkled under eyebrows snow white with the same liveliness as if she were still sixteen years old.

"To me!" she said again; and as he looked with undisguised ignorance of her meaning, it was impossible that she should not smile, and she hastily wiped away from the little eyes the tears that at first filled them. "Ah, you do not remember, my Father. It is a shame for a knight to forget a lady whose colors he has worn, — may a priest forget a lady whom he has served in the last extremity?" And she fairly laughed at his perplexity.

"Ah, Madame! you must pardon what time does, and exile. Whoever it is, I can see that you carry the secret of perpetual youth, but I lost that long ago. It is very long since I was in the castle of Montferrand, long before you were ever here, my lady."

"Chilperic will be ready before you guess me out," said she; "and, as your errand presses, I will tell you, if you will promise when it is over to stay as many weeks in the castle, as you have now spent minutes here. It is fair to remind you of the day when a girl with a scarlet cape, and a girl with a blue cape, and a girl with no cape at all, went sailing down the river with two young squires and with a very foolish page, from the home of the Barons of Braine. And have you forgotten — "

"Alix! Alix de Braine! It is impossible that I should have forgotten! But that you are here is as strange as that I am here. Where the four others are, perhaps you know!"

"Chilperic is ready, my Lord." This was the interruption of the groom at the door.

"Chilperic is ready, and life and death compel me to go on. Dear Lady Alix, you ask me to be your guest. You do not know, then, that if I had drunk from this cup of wine, you would share my excommunication; that if I slept under this roof, you could never enter church again; no, not to be borne there on your bier!"

"Did I not know it?" whispered the brave little woman. "Did I not know that you were journeying 'For the love of Christ,' and do not my husband and I beg you to stay with us as his guest and ours? Our request is made, and our welcome will be given

'In His Name.'"

And they parted.

The baron had already left the hall. When the priest stepped into the court-yard, and as he put his foot in the stirrup, he saw to his surprise that his host had already mounted another horse, and was waiting for him, himself ready equipped for a winter's expedition. A heavy fox-skin jacket had been thrown over the dress, none too light, which he wore before, and he had in the moment of his absence drawn on riding boots also.

The father acknowledged the courtesy, but expressed his unwillingness to give to his host such trouble. He was glad of his company, he said, but really he needed no protection.

"Protection! I think not, while

you are on or are near the territory of Montferrand." This was the baron's reply, with the addition of one or two rough oaths, untranslatable either into our language or into the habit of this page, but such as, it must be confessed, shot like a sort of lurid thread into the web-work of all the poor man's conversation. "I should not like to see poacher or peasant who would say a rough word to any man whom he saw riding on one of my horses. No, my father, it is not to protect you that I ride, but to talk with you. We hill barons are rough fellows, as I said, but we are not the clowns or the fools that the gentry of the chapter choose to think us. Meximieux here has tried to cheat me about the fish, and has sent his falcons after my herons a dozen times, so that I have not spoken to him or to his for fifteen years before he went off on this Holy Land tomfoolery,—I beg your reverence's pardon for calling it so. But I will say of Meximieux himself, that he is neither clown nor fool, and if I were to have to strike at King Saladin or any of his Emirs, I had rather Meximieux were at my side than any of the dandy-jacks I saw the day the bridge went down. We are rough fellows, I say,"—and here he tried to pick up the thread which he had dropped a long breath before, but he tried not wholly successfully,—"we are rough fellows, I say; but when a man of courage and of heart like your reverence comes to see us, and that is none too often, we are glad to learn something of what he has learned, and we would fain answer his questions if he have any to put to us."

"But I must say to you, my Lord, as I said to the Lady Alix, that to help me on my way is to put yourself under the ban. I was recognized within this hour by two of the monks in the abbey of Cornillon yonder, old and intimate friends of mine. Perhaps they will not denounce me, but the first fishermen we meet may, or the first shepherd's boy. For I have trudged up and down this valley too often for me to be a stranger here. It is not fair that I should expose you, for your courtesy, to the punishment which is none too easy upon me."

"Punishment be ——!" said the baron, with an oath again. Nor did the excellent man even condescend to the modern foolery of asking the clergyman's pardon for such excesses,—"it is no great punishment to a hill baron to tell him that he shall never enter a church. It is some little while since I have troubled them, even now. And if it should happen that this old carcass should rot on the hill-side where it happens to fall, why that is neither more nor less than is happening this very winter to many a gallant fellow who went on their fool's errand—I beg your pardon—against the Saracen. To tell the truth, sir, I want to talk about this very business,—of your punishment, as you call it, and of what I and other good fellows are to do, who hold that you and your friends are right, and that the soup-guzzling, wine-tippling, book-burning, devil-helping gowned men down in the city yonder are all wrong." It was with a good deal of difficulty that he worked through this long explanation, even with the help which his swearing seemed to give him. But there could be no doubt that he was very much in earnest in making it. He seemed to be helped by the tremendous pace at which the two horses, who had been caged in the stables for two or three days, were taking them over a stretch of level road.

"I do not know what I can tell you," said the priest, who seemed to be as little disturbed as the baron was by the rapidity of their pace, and rode as if he had been born on horseback. "I cannot tell you what to do, because I hardly know what I am to do myself — except wait. I wait till the good Lord shall open brighter days, as in His Day he will. Meanwhile, from day to day, I do what my hand finds to do, 'For the Love of Christ,' or

'In His Name.'"

"All very fine of you, my Father," said the other, a little chastened perhaps by his temperance of tone. "All very fine of you, who have something to do for the 'love of Christ.' You can go hither or thither, and every man has, as my wife Alix there had, some story to tell of the cure you have wrought or the comfort you have given. But that is nothing to me. It is not every day that I have a chance to beard the damned rascals in their own hell-hole. by giving a horse from my stables to one of these men they are hunting. I wish to God it were!" And the baron's rage rose so that he became unintelligible, as the horses forged along.

When the priest caught his drift again, he was saying, "If it had not been such damned nonsense, all nursery tales and chapman's stuff and priest's gabble, — I beg your pardon, sir,—I would have left the whole crew of them. Thirty men in good armor can I put on horseback, Sir Priest, and though they should not be all as well mounted as is your reverence, yet not one of the dogs should cross a beast but was better than those which that hog of a Meximieux rode and led, when he followed the Archbishop to the Holy Land. Enough better," he added, with a chuckle, "than that waddling oil-sack that I saw the Archbishop himself ambling out of Lyons upon. I tell you I would have gone to these wars gladly, if I could have thought there were fewer Archbishops in the armies, and more men with heads upon their shoulders. But I told Alix, said I, they are all fools that are not knaves, and all knaves that are not fools; and, if King Saladin eats them all, the world will be the better for it. No matter for them, your reverence. Now the Archbishop is gone, could not a few of us,— perhaps Servette yonder, Blon, I think, and very likely Montluel, no matter for names, — suppose we put two hundred good men in saddle, and take down as many more spearmen with tough ash lances. Suppose we raised a cross of our own, such a cross as this, your reverence," and he made the criss-cross sweep up and down, and then from right to left, by which all these affiliated men and women denoted the cross of Malta. Suppose we rode into Lyons some moonlight evening, shouting that we came "For the Love of Christ," do you not think that there are as many stout weavers and dock-men and boatmen, and other good fellows there, who would turn out

'In His Name'?"

Then when he saw that the priest did not answer, he added, "I tell you, Father, we would send their seneschals and their viguiers and their couriers and their popinjay men-at-arms scattering in no time; we would smoke the old pot bellies out of their kitchens and refectories, and we would bring the Poor Men of Lyons home to their own houses, to the House of Bread and the House of God, quite as quick as they were driven out." All this, with a scattered fire of wild oaths, which added to the droll incongruity of what the good fellow was saying.

If John of Lugio had been a mere ecclesiastic, he would have said, "Ah, my friend, they who take the sword must perish with the sword." And then the poor baron, who had perhaps never spoken at such length in his life before, would have shrunk back into his shell, cursed himself for a fool and his companion for another, and never would have understood why an offer so promising was refused. But John of Lugio was not a mere ecclesiastic, nor was he any other sort of fool. He was a man of God, indeed, but he showed in this case, as in a thousand others, as in his whole life he showed, that he knew how to tell God's messages to all sorts of men. "My Lord," said he, "perhaps you are right in thinking that these kings and barons and archbishops and bishops, and all the rest of the pilgrims who have gone to the Holy City, will never get there. Perhaps you are right in thinking that if they ride down fifty thousand Saracens and burn the houses of fifty thousand more, they will not teach the Saracens any very good lesson of God's love or of God's son. I believe you are right, or I would have gone when my old friend the Archbishop went. But suppose we rode into Lyons in the same fashion; suppose we drove out the chapter, as the chapter drove us out; suppose we stole their horses, as they stole ours,— why all the world would have a right to say worse things of the 'Poor Men of Lyons,' than it has ever said till now. No! no! my Lord," he said, after a moment; "leave it to time and to the good God above there. No fear that this archbishop will prosper too long, or this chapter; and for me, what more can I ask than as good a friend as I have found this day? And for you, what more can you ask than such a home as Montferrand, and such a wife as the Lady Alix?"

But the baron was hardly disposed to turn off, with a laugh, the plan which seemed to him so promising. He began upon it again; he even showed to his friend that he had thought it out in detail. He knew how large a guard was here and how large there; how many of the best men-at-arms were in Syria with the Archbishop; and how poor were the equipments of those who were left at home. "In old times," he said, "the Count of Forez would have been at our backs, but now, who knows but he would strike a stout blow on our side? There is not a man this side Marseilles who would be more glad than he to see these black-bellied hornets smoked out of their hives."

The Father listened as courteously as before, but as firmly. He seemed to think that a little authority might well be exerted now, and he said simply: "My Lord. I warn you that you are thinking of what you must not think of If what you propose were the right thing to do, you would have been warned of it before now by those in authority. Till you are, and till I am, we must let monks, priests, and bishops alone."

And Montferrand supposed, perhaps he supposed rightly, that somewhere the "Poor Men of Lyons" had a council and a master, wiser than he was, who would some day give him a signal when he might gallop on this road on the back of Chilperic, with every man whom he could put in the saddle, ready for a raid into Lyons. The baron was not yet trained enough in trusting Providence to know that the only authority to which John of Lugio would ever defer, was an authority far above chapter, archbishop, king, or pope.

He turned the subject, therefore, a little uneasily, to the eternal question of the crusade. Did his reverence think the troopers would soon be home again? and did he think they would find the sword of Saladin so weak? and all the other questions of the home gossip of the day. Meanwhile, on all the road which did not absolutely forbid speed, the two horses flew along, much as Barbe Noire had flown that morning, and with no such fatal issue. The ride was a short one, indeed, before they entered the court-yard of the Castle of Meximieux. Here was the horse of Gualtier of the Mill, saddled, bridled, and waiting for his rider.

"Sixteen years since I saw the inside of this court!" said Montferrand, as he swung himself off his horse, and as he wiped his forehead. "The tall tree yonder has been planted since then. As I remember the court, my man, there was not a green twig in it."

The servant bowed, and said that the trees which the baron saw had all been there when he came into the stable service, but, as the baron saw, they were not very old.

"Sixteen years!" said the rugged old chief again. "It was fifteen years ago at Michaelmas that I asked Meximieux if he would make the fish good to me, and he swore he would do no such thing. And I have not spoken to him from that day to this. And now he is lying under some fig-tree yonder, and I am standing in his castle court. Your reverence, I should have said this morning, that all the devils in hell could not bring me into the shadow of Meximieux's walls. And see what you have done."

"Ah, my lord," said the other, who had already mounted; "a messenger from heaven, though he be a very humble one, can do a great deal that the devils in hell cannot do. And now, my lord, good-by. Give a poor priest's best salutations to the Lady Alix. And, my lord, when Meximieux comes home, win a greater victory than he has done. Ask him if, 'For the love of Christ,' he will not make it right about the fish, and see what a pilgrim like him will answer, 'In His Name.'"

He gave the baron his hand, and was gone. "As good a horseman," said the old man, "as ever served under King Philip. And I wonder how many of them all are doing as good service as he is this day!"

Gualtier of the Mill had not exaggerated the worth of the horse which the priest mounted, and the horse had never had a better rider. From Meximieux to Lyons, the road was and is more than seven leagues, but the rider knew that it was by far the easier part of the way, and, thanks to Chilperic and the baron, he had left full half the time allotted for his journey. He had the hope also, which proved well founded, that he might not have to rely on the miller's horse alone, but that he might find at Miribel, or some other village on the road, a fresh horse sent out to meet him by Jean Waldo.

In this hope, he rode faster than he would have dared to do, were he obliged to use one horse for the whole journey. And at a rapid rate, indeed, and without companionship or adventure, he came to the hamlet which the miller had left that morning, where poor Prinhac's enterprise had come to a conclusion so untimely. The horse neighed his recognition of some of his companions, as they entered the wretched hamlet, and, in a moment more, the father saw Prinhac himself, evidently waiting for him, in the shadow of the wall of the miller's garden.

The weaver stepped forward into the roadway as John of Lugio approached, and, with his little willow switch, made in the air the mystic sign. The priest drew bridle, and the horse evidently knew that he was at home. Prinhac and the priest had never met before. The weaver eagerly asked the other if he were the physician so much desired, and thanked God as eagerly when he knew that, so far, his mission had not been in vain. "I would break my collar-bone a dozen times, if I could save my young mistress so easily. And there is not another boy on the looms or in the shops but would say the same thing." He told the priest hastily that he knew little about the girl's disaster. He described to him his own route and progress, and the miserable accident by which he had been delayed. He added, "Nothing was said about fresh horses, but I have been watching for them all day. You ought to meet some one at Miribel, or, at the worst, when you cross the river the first time."

The priest asked him what he could tell him about the girl's illness.

"Nothing — nothing. I know she was as well as a bird at sunset; I saw her and spoke to her as she came singing down the hill. The next I knew was, that my master woke me in the dead of the dark, and asked me for the love of Christ to bring to you this message. Forgive me, father, but if he had asked me to do it for love of Mademoiselle Félicie, I should have done it as willingly."

"Hast thou done it unto one of the least of these, thou hast done it unto me!" Such was the half answer of the priest, which, perhaps, the crippled weaver understood. "I must not stay, my good fellow; if I am to be of any use, I must go. I shall tell the child how faithful a messenger she found in you. God bless you, and farewell."

The weaver was right in supposing that a relay would await the physician at Miribel. He found there another of Jean Waldo's men with another of his horses. The man did not, of course, recognize the physician, nor the horse he rode; but it was not difficult for the priest, who was on the lookout for him, to persuade him that it was for him that Cœur-Blanc had been saddled. The man had left Lyons two hours before noon. His tidings of his young mistress were scarcely encouraging. She was no better, he was sure of that. The Florentine doctor had not left her all the day, nor her father or mother; he was sure of that. His directions were simply to wait for the priest at Miribel, and to bid him mount Cœur-Blanc, while he was to bring home Barbe-Noire as soon as might be. So

The Father rode on alone. The child was alive. So far was well. For the rest, he had carried with him all day that sinking of heart which any man feels when he is called to struggle with death, only because all others have so far failed in that very encounter.

CHAPTER VI.

THE TROUBADOUR.

Freshly mounted, and well mounted too, the tired man bade the groom good-by, and entered on his last hour with that comfortable feeling which, even to the most tired man, the last hour brings. Alas! it was the old story, Prinhac's story of the morning. He was, as it proved, in more danger in this last hour, than he had been through all the rest of the day.

He was pushing over the meadows of the valley at a sharp trot, when he met a rider coming out from the city, on a sorry-looking beast, in the rather jaunty or fantastic costume which indicated that he was one of the trouvères, or troubadours. The man nodded good-naturedly, perhaps a little familiarly. John of Lugio, absorbed in the old-time memories which the day had renewed, acknowledged the salutation with less familiarity, but with a sort of reserved courtesy, taking, indeed, but little real notice of the traveller as he did so. The man pushed on cheerfully, but, in a moment, stopped his horse, turned, and scrutinized the priest with care, and then making a speaking trumpet of both hands, hailed him with:—

"Holà! holà! there; will you halt a minute?"

Halting was not in John of Lugio's schedule for that afternoon, if he could help himself. He heard the cry distinctly, but knew no reason why he should stop at the demand of a troubadour. On the other hand, he would not seem to avoid the other. He did not turn for an instant, therefore; he did not spur his horse on the other hand, but he let him hold to the sharp, rapid trot that he was pursuing.

The troubadour saw his haste, and shouted only with the more eagerness: —

"Holà! holà! there; halt! halt!"

But the well-mounted rider swept along.

The stranger screamed once more, but saw that the other halted his speed not by a second. He was, indeed, out of any fair ear-shot by this time.

The troubadour fairly groaned. He looked anxiously at the declining sun, and resolved, on the instant, to go in pursuit of the fugitive, even with the wretched brute which he had under him, who was but the poorest competitor in a match with Jean Waldo's powerful Arab on which the priest was mounted.

For the priest himself, he did not once turn round. It was not his part to show anxiety, and, indeed, he did not know that he was followed. But, if he were followed, he did not mean to be readily overtaken.

There is a little elevation in the road, as it crosses the slope of a spur of one of the northern hills, and the moment that John of Lugio knew that he was shielded by it from the sight of any one on the flat ground behind, he pressed his horse even to a gallop, and flew over the ground at a speed which almost defied pursuit. Had this rate of going lasted he would soon have found himself at the Rhone again.

But no; he had to draw bridle in less than a mile, that his unusual rate of travel might not challenge the curiosity of the loungers in a little hamlet before him as the road turned. Two or three horses were tethered on the outside of a wine-shop, a boy seemed to be watching them, and one or two idlers stood by. John of Lugio hoped that he might get by without attracting attention.

No! As he nodded civilly to the by-standers, two men, half soldiers, half gens-d'armes, if these modern words explain at all a race of officers now existing no longer, stepped out from the tavern. They were in the livery worn by the servants of police of the archbishop and chapter of Lyons.

"Where's your haste, my tall friend?" said the one who was rather the more tipsy of the two. "Where's your haste to-day? Stop and have something — something to drink with Jean Gravier here. His wine is bad, the worst wine I ever drank, but it is better wine than none."

The priest's business at this moment was, not to preach, nor warn, nor convert drunkards from the error of their ways, but to get to Lyons before sunset. He showed no sign of annoyance, but laughed good-naturedly, and said, —

"Thank you kindly; I will pay the scot if the rest will drink. But I have but just mounted at Miribel yonder, and I must be in Lyons before the sun goes down."

"Sun!" said the drunken tipstaff, "sun be hanged! The sun has two good hours yet in the sky, and with that horse of yours, you will see the guard long before sunset. Come and try Jean Gravier's red wine."

The priest would not show uneasiness. But again he declined, proposing that a stoup of wine should be brought out that all the company might share; judging, not unwisely, that he should do well to enlist as many of them as he might upon his side. At this, another of the officers came out from the tavern. Unfortunately for the priest's errand, he was much more sober than his companion. Unfortunately again, he was no foreign hireling, as the others were, but was a Lyonnais born. The moment he looked upon John of Lugio he recognized him, or thought he did, and he addressed him in a mood very different from that of his noisy companions. The man looked jealously at Father John, as men of his craft were and are apt to look at all strangers. He did not drop or turn his eye either; after the first glance he surveyed the whole figure of the rider, and his horse as well.

"You are riding one of Jean Waldo's horses," he said, gruffly.

"I am," said the priest; "he sent it out to meet me by one of his grooms. I left my own horse at Miribel."

"You are a friend of Jean Waldo's, then?"

"I am a friend of a friend of his," said the priest, with an aspect of courage and frankness, "and I am eager to be in Lyons at to-morrow's festival at his house. That is why I cannot tarry with our friends here. I must pay my scot and begone."

"Not quite so fast," said the officer; "have you any pass to show if you are asked for one at the bridge?"

"Pass, — no," said the priest, laughing. "I had a pass years ago, signed by the Viguier, but it was worn out long since, while I waited for somebody to ask me for it I think the Viguier will not turn out any of Jean Waldo's friends. What is my scot?" he said, as if impatient, to the tavern-keeper. "All the passes in the world will not serve me if I come to the long bridge after sundown. And I should be glad to be there before the crowd."

The tavern-keeper took the copper coins which the priest paid him, and Father John, on his part, saluted the others, and turned as if he would go away, when the persistent officer stopped him.

"Not so fast, my friend. You know very well that I have good right to question you, and you must not wonder if I suspect you. If you take a little ride to-night with me and my friends here to the chateau of Meyzieux where we are going, I promise you as good a bed there as Messer Jean Waldo will give you. Then you can ride into Lyons with us in the morning, and can make a little visit to the Viguier with me, before you go to your Christmas dinner. That will give him a chance to give you another parchment pass, and I am quite sure he will be glad to do so, unless he wants your closer company.

And he gave a loud guffaw of laughter, in which his two companions joined.

For the peasants and the tavern-keeper, they were too much accustomed to such acts of petty tyranny on the part of petty officials to show surprise. Indeed, they hardly felt it. John of Lugio knew that, though he might have their sympathy, they would not render to him any sort of help if he defied in the least the authority of his persecutors.

With that same unperturbed manner which he had shown all along, he laughed good-naturedly, and said at once, what was perfectly true: —

"The Viguier is an old friend of mine, and will remember me very well." Then he added, "Suppose I meet you and your friends as you come into town to-morrow, and go round there and see him. I give you my hand on it that I will be at the drawbridge at any time you name."

And he offered his bare hand.

"No," said the other, sternly and slowly. "We are not such fools as to take men's hands, unless to put handcuffs on them. You will go to Meyzieux with us in half an hour. Till then you may come into the house and drink with us, or you may stay out here and freeze, as it pleases you. Michel, Antoine, keep your eyes on him, and see that he does not leave." And he turned to go into the tavern. But he saw that the priest made no resistance. On the other hand, he dismounted at once, and occupied himself in looking for something which had clogged the shoe of the noble horse which he was riding.

At this moment the attention of all parties was engaged by the arrival of a new-comer upon the scene. The surly officer himself loitered on the steps of the inn, when he heard the clear, loud voice of the troubadour: —

"Who will listen yet again
To the old and jovial strain,
The old tale of love that 's ever new?
She 's a girl as fair as May,
He 's a boy as fresh as day,
And the story is as gay as it is true."

The voice was a perfectly clear and pure tenor. The air was lively without being rapid, and the enunciation and emphasis of the singer were perfect. The poor beast he rode came panting into the crowd, his sides wet and dirty; and the singer, with undisguised satisfaction, sprang from his back, and threw the rein to a stable-boy.

"Your servant, gentlemen, — your servant, gentlemen, — are there no lovers of the gay science in this honorable company?" And in that clear, powerful tone he began again:

"Who will hear the pretty tale
Of my thrush and nightingale, —
Of the dangers and the sorrows that he met?
How he fought without a fear
For his charming little dear,
Aucassin and his loving Nicolette."

"A beautiful song, and a story that will make you laugh and make you cry, gentlemen, both together.

"Will you hear the pretty tale, or is it too gay for you? We are not always gay. We trouvèurs have fathers and mothers and sisters and brothers like the rest of you. We have to lay our little babies in the ground sometimes, as you do." All this he said perfectly seriously and reverently. "We love the good God as you love him, and we can tell you the stories of the saints and of the prophets; may God bless us all as we do so."

And then in a minor key, and with a strain wholly different, he sang slowly, and almost in tears it seemed,—

"For the Love of Christ our Saviour along the road I came,
And what I stop to sing you, I sing it IN HIS NAME."

It need hardly be said that John of Lugio caught the indication given to him, that this was a friend, from whom he had been so rashly escaping. The poor brute before him was still panting from the efforts which the rider had made to overtake Cœur-Blanc before he reached the trap into which the priest had fallen. In that the singer had failed. But none the less had he bravely pressed on and entered that trap himself. And by the little scrap he sang, he revealed himself as a friend to the other,—one friend who could be relied upon in the midst of indifferent spectators and avowed enemies. John of Lugio did not dare reply, even by a glance. The singer needed no reply, and looked for no glance. He went on, as they all sat down in the one room of the tavern, as if he were rattling on in the fashion of his craft: —

"Or I have the new song, which won the golden violet last year.

"In a pretty little meadow, in a country that I know,
A pretty little flower did bourgeon and did grow,
Its root was in a dunghill, but day to day would bring
Fresh food and fragrance to the weed, all through the days of spring."

His clear resonant voice was fairly triumphant as the words rolled on. But he stopped and said, "Boy, bring me my little guitar; if I am to sing to the gentlemen, I must play to them too. Only tell me what it shall be, gentlemen."

"Let it be," said John of Lugio, boldly, "the song you sing 'For the Love of Christ and in His Name.'" And thus he opened his communication with the other.

The chief of the officers turned with an undisguised sneer upon his prisoner. "So, said he, we are coming the godly, are we? That's old chaff for such as we, Mr. Friend's friend. Sing one of your love songs."

"Love songs be hanged!" said the keeper of the inn; "the girls here say they have heard about Nicolette and Aucassin till they are tired; they want the new song, the song of the violet. Can you teach it to them, Messer Trouvèur?"

"I can sing it, and I can teach it too, to such apt scholars as Mademoiselle Anne," said the singer, rising and bowing as the buxom girl came into the room rather shyly, with one or two of her village companions. The troubadour, with some exercise of authority, cleared a place for them where he sate himself, — made the boys rise from their seats on a settle that the young women might have them, ran over the air once or twice on the guitar, and sang again.

THE SONG OF THE VIOLET OF GOLD.

I.

In a pretty little meadow in a country that I know,
A pretty little flower did bourgeon and did grow,
Its root was in a dunghill, but every day would bring
Fresh food and fragrance for the flower, all through the days of spring.
But when the spring was over, and because it was not strong,
The cruel wind came winding down, and did it wretched wrong,
And then came winter's frost, and stretched it on the earth
Above the dirty dunghill on which it had its birth.

II.

By the pretty little meadow beneath the sunny skies,
Is meant this wicked world of ours which lures us with its lies,
For evil takes away the light of life from me and you,
And brings us wicked tales to tell, and naughty deeds to do.
We live along our little lives all foolish and forlorn,
Nor turn to look a minute on the place where we were born,
So comes it that through winding ways in which our souls are tried,
We stumble stupid onward, with wickedness for guide.

III.

I say the little flower, which in the meadow grew,
Grew fair and then grew foul, just like me and just like you:
We 're gayly clad and bravely fed, when first our lives begin,
Before the enemy of man seduces us to sin.
So God has made the sight of heaven above the sunny sky,
As the blue flowers of spring-time bloom bright before the eye;
But then the fool of petty pride forgets where he was born,
And dies the death of sinful shame, all foolish and forlorn.

IV.

And the dunghill where the flower did flourish and did fade,
Is the dust of earth from which the Lord our father Adam made,
His children's children lived the lives of sinfulness and shame
From which the breath of being to our fathers' fathers came.
We climb the mountains high, and valleys low descend,
We toil and moil, and crowd with care our lives unto the end;
And when we die, all this we have is treasure thrown away,
And nothing 's left us for the tomb, except a clod of clay.

V.

The cruel wind which bent the flower and crushed it like a weed,
I say, is grasping pride of life, — is avarice and greed,
Which teaches us to hide our heads, and steal and cheat and lie,
And so it is that wicked folks torment us till we die.
And then, again, this winter wild which sweeps away the flower,
I say is false and cruel Death exulting in his power.
He grasps us in his hard embrace until all life is fled,
And throws us on the dunghill, when he knows our flesh is dead.[1]

The girls were nodding to the air, and were much more interested in that, perhaps, than in the words, — but the leader of the gens d'armes, if we may again use the modern word, expressed his scorn for the whole.

"Bring him some wine, Jean; wet his whistle for him.' Dunghills and Death, indeed, is that the best he has to sing of? Give him some wine, and give me some; give everybody some. Mr. Friend's friend's friend, take some wine to show you bear no malice. Girls! have some wine; all drink, and then let him tell us his love story."

With a good deal of bustle and readjustment of the company, with much fuss at serving wine for so many, these arbitrary orders were executed. The troubadour, meanwhile, was thrumming on his guitar, — tuning it, — and striking chords, or trying one or another bit of the tune. When the Captain gave word, at last, that they were all ready, he began again with the same song, with which he had at first arrested their attention: —

I.

Who will listen yet again
To the old and jovial strain,
The old tale of love that 's always new?
She 's a girl that 's fair as May,
He 's a boy as fresh as day,
And the story is as gay as it is true.

II.

Who will hear the pretty tale
Of my thrush and nightingale,—
Of the dangers and the sorrows that they met?
How he fought without a fear,
For his charming little dear,
Aucassin, and his loving Nicolette.

III.

For, my lords, I tell you true
That you never saw or knew,
Man or woman so ugly or so gray,
Who would not all day long
Sit and listen to the song
And the story that I tell you here to-day.

"THE STORY OF NICOLETTE AND AUCASSIN."

"Now you must know, my lords and my ladies, that the Count Bougars of Valence chose to make war with the Count Garin of Beaucaire. And the war was so cruel, that the Count never let one day go by, but what he came thundering at the walls and barriers of the town, with a hundred knights and with ten thousand men-at-arms, on foot and on horseback, who burned all the horses, and stole all the sheep, and killed all the people that they could.

"Now the Count Garin de Beaucaire was very old, and was sadly broken with years. He had used his time very ill, had the Count de Beaucaire. And the old wretch had no heir, either son or daughter, except one boy whose name was

AUCASSIN.

[1] The author hastens to admit the anachronism of introducing here this little poem. It received the Violet of Gold in the year 1345.

"Aucassin was gentle and handsome. He was tall and well made; his legs were good and his feet were good, his body was good and his arms were good. His hair was blond, a little curly; his eyes were like gray fur, for they were near silver and near blue, and they laughed when you looked at them. His nose was high and well placed; his face was clear and winning. Yes, and he had everything charming, and nothing bad about him. But this young man was so wholly conquered by love, — who conquers everybody, — that he would not occupy himself in any other thing. He would not be a knight, he would not take arms, he would not go to the tourneys, he would not do any of the things he ought to do.

"His father was very much troubled by this, and he said to him one morning: —

"'My son, take your arms, mount your horse, defend your country, protect your people. If they only see you in the midst of them, this will give them more courage; they will fight all the better for their lives and their homes; for your land and mine.

"'Father,' said Aucassin, 'why do you say this to me?

"'May God never hear my prayers, if I ever mount horse, or go to tourney, or to battle, before you have, yourself, given to me my darling Nicolette, — my sweetheart whom I love so dearly.

"'My son,' said the father to him, 'this cannot be.

"'Give up forever your dreams of this captive girl, whom the Saracens brought from some strange land, and sold to the Viscount here.

"'He trained her; he baptized her; she is his god-child.

"'Some day he will give her to some brave fellow who will have to gain his bread by his sword.

"'But you, my son, when the time comes that you wish to take a wife, I will give you some king's daughter, or at least the daughter of a Count.

"'There is not, in all Provence, a man so rich that you may not marry his daughter, if you choose.

"So said the old man. But Aucassin replied: —

"'Alas, my father; there is not in this world the principality which would not be honored if my darling Nicolette, my sweetest, went to live there.

"'If she were Queen of France or of England; if she were Empress of Germany or of Greece, she could not be more courteous or more gracious; she could not have sweeter ways or greater virtues.'"

At this point the troubadour nodded to the girl Anne, who, as she had said, knew the airs and the songs of the little Romance. One of the village girls joined her, and thus in trio the three sang: —

All the night and all the day
Aucassin would beg and pray:
"O, my father, give my Nicolette to me."
Then his mother came to say:
"What is it that my foolish boy can see?"
— "Nicolette is sweet and gay."

"But Nicolette 's a slave.
If a wife my boy would have,
Let him choose a lady fair of high degree."
"O, no; my mother, no!
For I love my darling so.
Her face is always bright
And her footstep 's always light,
And I cannot let my dainty darling go!
No, mother dear, she rules my heart!
No, mother dear, we cannot part!"

The commander of the squad of policemen had not mistaken in his estimate of the attractive powers of fiction, sentiment, and religion in such an assembly as that around the tavern. As the little love story went on with the song belonging to it, groups of idlers out-doors pressed into the great doorway of the tavern. The grooms left with the horses arranged that one boy only should hold them all; and he, getting hint of what was passing, made shift to knot the bridles together, to fasten them all to a halter at the corner of the house, and to crowd in after the rest. From the other cottage, which was used as a kitchen in the establishment, two or three more women appeared, — older than Anne and her companions, — and for these, as before, seats were provided on a settle. This last arrangement made a little delay, but so soon as the women were seated, the brisk troubadour went on.

"When the Count Garin of Beaucaire saw that he could not drag Nicolette out from the heart of Aucassin, he went to find the Viscount, who was his vassal, and he said to him: —

"'Sir Viscount, we must get rid of your god-child, Nicolette.

"'Cursed be the country where she was born, for she is the reason why I am losing my Aucassin, who ought to be a knight and who refuses to do what he ought to do.

"'If I can catch her, I will burn her at the stake, and I will burn you too.'

"'My Lord,' replied the Viscount, 'I am very sorry for what has happened, but it is no fault of mine.

"'I bought Nicolette with my money; I trained her; I had her baptized, and she is my god-child.

"'I wanted to marry her to a fine young man of mine, who would gladly have earned her bread for her, which is more than your son Aucassin could do.

"'But since your wish and your pleasure are what they are, I will send this god-child of mine away to such a land in such a country that Aucassin shall never set his eyes upon her again.'"

The little audience of the troubadour, quite unused to "sensation" of this sort, many of them fresh as children to the charm of a well-told story, pressed closer and closer to him. With the rarest of gifts, and that least possible to gain by study, the trouvèur fairly talked to them in tones of perfect conversational familiarity. His eyes caught sympathizing eyes as he glanced from side to side of the room, and his animation quickened, and his words became more confidential. At last, indeed, he addressed himself personally to the Captain; when he was fully satisfied that, in the confusion which accompanied the entrance of the women, John of Lugio had risen from his quiet seat behind the inner door, and had, unnoticed, left the room.

The troubadour continued in his most confidential narrative tone, —

"'See that you do so,' cried the Count Garin to the Viscount, 'or great misfortunes will come to you.'

"So saying, he left his vassal.

"Now the Viscount had a noble palace, of high walls, surrounded by a thickly planted garden. He put Nicolette into one of the rooms of this palace, in the very highest story.

"She had an old woman for her only companion, with enough bread and meat and wine, and everything else that they needed to keep them alive.

"Then he fastened and concealed

the door, so that no one could go in, and he left no other opening but the window, which was very narrow and opened on the garden."

Again the story-teller nodded to the two girls, and they sang all together.

Nicolette was put in prison ;
  And a vaulted room
Wonderfully built and painted
  Was her prison-home.

The pretty maiden came
To the marble window-frame ;
  Her hair was light,
  Her eyes were bright,
And her face was a charming face to see.
  No ; never had a knight
A maid with such a charming face to see.

  She looked into the garden close
  And there she saw the open rose,
  Heard the thrushes sing and twitter,
  And she sang in accent bitter :
O, why am I a captive here ?
  Why locked up in cruel walls ?
Aucassin, my sweetheart dear,
  Whom my heart its master calls,
I have been your sweetheart for this live-
      long year !
  That is why I've come
  To this vaulted room,
But by God, the son of Mary, no !
I will not be captured so,
If only I can break away, and go !

Then the troubadour continued :—

"So Nicolette was put in prison, as you have just heard, and soon a cry and noise ran through the country that she was lost. Some said that she had run away ; others said that the Count Garin de Beaucaire had killed her.

"All in despair at the joy which this news seemed to cause to some people, Aucassin went to find the viscount of the town.

"'Lord Viscount,' he asked him, 'what have you done with Nicolette, my sweetest love, the thing in all the world which I love best ?

"'You have stolen her !

"'Be sure, Viscount, that if I die of this, the blame shall fall on you.

"'For, surely, it is you who tear away my life in tearing away my darling Nicolette !

"'Fair sir,' answered the Viscount, 'do let this Nicolette alone, for she is not worthy of you ; she is a slave whom I have bought with my deniers, and she must serve as a wife to a young fellow of her own state, to a poor man, and not to a lord like you, who ought to marry none but a king's daughter, or at least a Count's daughter.

"'What should you be doing for yourself if you did make a lady of this vile creature, and marry her?

"'Then would you be very happy, indeed, very happy, for your soul would abide forever in hell. And never should you enter into paradise.'

"'Into Paradise?' repeated Aucassin, angrily. 'And what have I to do there? I do not care to go there if it be not with Nicolette, my sweetest darling whom I love so much.'

"'Into Paradise! And do you know who those are that go there, you who think it is a place where I must wish to go? They are old priests, old cripples, old one-eyed men, who lie day and night before the altars, sickly, miserable, shivering, half naked, half fed ; dead already before they die! These are they who go to paradise, and they are such pitiful companions that I do not desire to go to paradise with them.'

"'But to hell would I gladly go ; for to hell go the good clerks and the fair knights slain in battle and in great wars ; the brave Sergeants-at-Arms and the men of noble lineage. And with all these would I gladly go.'

"'Stop,' says the Viscount; 'all which you can say and nothing at all, are exactly the same thing; never shall you see Nicolette again.

"'What you and I may get for this, would not be pleasant, if you still will be complaining.

"'We all might be burned by your father's command,—Nicolette, you, and I myself into the bargain.'

"'I am in despair!' murmured Aucassin, leaving the Viscount, who was no less angry than himself."

The company gathered nearer and nearer together, eager not to lose one word. Nor was any one roused from the interest of the story, till a new traveller stopped at the wretched tavern.

"Holà! holà!" he cried. "Is there no one to care for my horse?"

Antoine, the stable-boy, rushed out, and to his shame and horror all the horses were gone.

But with the agony and falsehood of despair, he took the stranger's horse, as if nothing had happened, and said to him: —

"I will see to the horse, Monsieur, give yourself no care. Will you step into the house? There is the best trouvère singing there, who travels all over this country. He is telling the story of Nicolette.

"I will take good care of your horse, sir; never fear me."

For poor Antoine's only fear was, that the master of the newly arrived beast would stay outside.

In fact that worthy did loiter a moment, and gave one or two directions about his horse. Poor Antoine was dying to ask him if he met five saddled horses as he came. But he did not dare disgrace himself; and he thought, wisely enough, that if the stranger had seen any such cavalcade, he would surely have mentioned it.

At last, by repeated solicitation, he induced the man to enter the tavern, and, with solicitude wholly unusual, the stable-boy drew the door to, after the traveller had passed in. He could hear the trio again, as the two girls joined with the troubadour.

But the poor stable-boy cursed Nicolette and Aucassin both, with adjurations and anathemas which they had never learned, and wished all troubadours were on the other side of the sea. If those horses could not be brought back before his master, or before the Viguier's officer found they were gone, he, Antoine, would be well flogged before he went to bed. That was certain. No Christmas holiday for him, — that was certain also. And whether, at the beginning of a cold winter, he were not put in handcuffs and carried to one of those horrid prisons which he had heard the officers talking of; of this the frightened boy was by no means certain.

So soon as he had closed the door, instead of leading the hot and wet beast, intrusted to him, to the stable, as he knew he should do, he fastened him by the rein firmly but quickly, and at his best speed ran up the road, where he might gain the view from the hill, and get a survey of the whole meadow.

"For the cursed brutes," he said, "are all fastened together, wherever they have gone."

And then he reflected, with profound satisfaction, that the tale of Nicolette and Aucassin was very long, — or that one of the girls had told him so in a whisper. Perhaps they would stay in the tavern longer than the Captain had said, if only the troubadour could make it entertaining enough.

Ah! Antoine, you need not fear the troubadour! He is making it as entertaining as he knows how,— and that is what he is there for,— that he may keep them all for the precious minutes that shall take Cœur-Blanc into Lyons.

So Antoine pressed up the road to the little swell of land over which it passed, from which, as he approached, John of Lugio had first seen the group standing at the tavern

The poor boy came up the hill, all out of breath, and scanned the wide meadows. A few cows here; a stray traveller or two there; clouds of dust on the highway, which might conceal this or that or something else,—who should say? But no definite sign of the horses.

The wretched boy climbed a tree; but he only lost time, and saw nothing. He could see that Philip of Fontroyes, the lame man, was hobbling home with his sorry cow.

The boy rushed to meet Philip. Philip was very deaf, and, like other dull people, could not answer the square question put to him, till he knew who he was that asked it, why he asked it, and for what purpose he asked it. When he was at last secure on these points, he ventured to say, —

"Horses, no horses; no, no horses. There was a span of mules that a man with a red jerkin drove by, that was two hours ago. But no horses."

As Antoine knew that if Philip had had any eye, or any memory, he must have reported at least the passage of Cœur-Blanc, and that of the troubadour, and that of the stranger whom he had just left; three horses, certainly; this assurance that no horses had passed on the road was anything but encouraging.

Poor boy! he looked back a moment on the tavern; he thought of the pretty, pleasant way in which Lulu had spoken to him only that morning, and of the blue ribbon he had ready to give to her the next day; he thought, shall we confess it in this connection, of his own feast-day suit of clothes, which were in his box in the wretched attic where he slept.

But he thought also of the flogging which was so sure if he were detected. He would never see Lulu again, nor his gay garments again! He looked his last on the tavern, and fled along the high road — away from it and from Lyons — as fast as his feet could carry him.

The troubadour, who saw everything, saw or knew or felt or comprehended the entrance of the newcomer, and heard Antoine as he closed the outer door of the tavern. The troubadour did not pause a moment in his story. The stranger, with a courteous gesture, intimated that he would not interrupt it, and took the seat by the great fire, which Dame Gravier, with a good deal of fuss and pretence of hospitality, cleared for him.

The Captain of the officers started, as if he had perhaps dozed a little in the last refrain of the singers, but really gave some attention to the story-teller, as he went on without any pause —as the story required him to do — after another little song:—

Then Aucassin went home,
But his heart was wrung with fear
By the parting from his dainty dear:
His dainty dear so fair,
Whom he sought for everywhere,
But nowhere could he find her, far or near.

To the palace he has come,
  And he climbs up every stair, —
He hides him in his room
  And weeps in his despair.

"O, my Nicolette," said he,
"So dear and sweet is she!
  So sweet for that, so sweet for this,
  So sweet to speak, so sweet to kiss,
 So sweet to come, so sweet to stay,
 So sweet to sing, so sweet to play,
  So sweet when there, so sweet when here,
  O, my darling! O, my dear,
  Where are you, my sweet? while I
  Sit and weep so near to die,
 Because I cannot find my darling dear."[1]

To a modern ear it is difficult to give the impression of the effect of the long closing line, as the three voices, in strict unison, closed the little song, — with perfect spirit, running up rapidly in a whole octave, and closing an octave higher than the key-note, to which they would naturally have returned.

The narrative then continued: —

"Meanwhile, I can tell you, the fighting went on. For the Count Bougars pressed hard on the Count Garin. He had a thousand men-at-arms in one camp, and he had a thousand in another. And while Aucassin was shut up in his chamber, and lamenting his dear Nicolette, the Count was bringing up great battering-rams to hammer down the walls of the city."

"Ah, yes," grunted the Captain, "let us hear about the battering-rams. I was sergeant in a battering-train at Gron, myself, I was!" And he drank off another good draught from his tankard, and then droppng back in his chair, gave attention in the manner of those people, who can hear a preacher better when their eyes are closed.

"He brought up one battering-ram, with a very brave sergeant in charge of it, on one side the city; and, on another side, he brought up another with two counts, and a duke in charge of it.

"At last he thought all was ready, and on each side of the town he gathered all his footmen and all his horsemen for the assault."

"What did he want horsemen for, to storm a breach with?" growled the sergeant.

"I beg your honor's pardon," said the trouvère, who had not made the blunder without a purpose. "But the troubadour who told this story to me had not seen so many sieges as your honor."

"I should think not; I should think not," grunted the drunken critic, well satisfied with the success of his interruption, and the trouvère continued as confidentially as before, and as if the sergeant was his only auditor.

"Everybody in the city was called to arms to defend the walls. They supposed that the attack would be made on the eastern side, because the breach was there."

"Yes, yes," grunted the experienced soldier, "of course the attack would be made where the breach was."

And he nodded complacently upon the inn-keeper and upon his own companions, as if he would say, "Of course we know more of war than these singing fellows do."

The troubadour continued: —

"The principal attacking party might have gone quite wrong had it been left to the dukes, but the brave fellow I told you of before —"

[1] The original is very pretty, and can be guessed out, even by the unlearned reader: —

"Nicolete biax esters,
 Biax venir et biax alers
 Biax déduis et dous parlers,
 Biax borders et biax jouers,
 Biax baisiers, biax acolers."

And it is impossible to tell what wonders the sergeant on his side might have wrought, or the duke and the count on theirs, in vain rivalry with a sergeant so puissant. For at this fatal moment, the horse whom Antoine had left to freeze, thinking it was quite time that his needs should be attended to, gave an ominous neigh.

"Neigh-eigh-eigh-eigh."

The sound rang through the crowded room; and Jean the inn-keeper himself started from his seat and looked around, and, seeing that all the servants were rushing out-doors, followed them. The master of the horse of course followed, and the officers; and the troubadour and the girls were left in the confusion alone.

"Where's Antoine? where's Antoine?" Cries of Antoine! Antoine! resounded everywhere. To tell the truth, the tavern was not unused to such clamor. Poor Antoine was the man-of-all-work, always summoned.

"Don't come out into the cold, sir!" said Jean Gravier, perfectly used to making up the scanty resources of his wretched tavern by the boldest lying. "Go back into the inn, if you please. My wife has supper ready. Antoine has taken the horses to water them."

"Water them!" said the stranger, with an oath; "and why has he not taken mine to groom him and give him a bed, as he said he would? The beast is wellnigh frozen already, while you and your people are singing your love-songs."

"Certainly, certainly," said Jean Gravier, "I shall rub him down myself." And he led the poor wretch to the stable, wondering where Antoine was with the other horses, and beckoning to Ode, one of the hangers-on, to follow.

"Jean Gravier, come back; what is all this row about, and what are you doing with the horses of the honorable men-at-arms of the Bishop and Chapter of Lyons?"

With many oaths, some hiccough, and other interruptions, the Captain of the policemen, standing upon the step, thus hailed the tavern-keeper.

Jean Gravier pretended not to hear.

"Come back, you dog, come back, and answer to the charge made against you." This was the second appeal of the drunken fool, who doubted a little his own ability to run after the delinquent vintner, and made up in grandeur of words for whatever failure of bodily force he was conscious of.

Jean Gravier did not dare go on.

"For God's sake, find the horses, Ode. Send Pierre up the road, and send Andre down; unless, indeed, which God grant, that brute of an Antoine has had the grace to put them all into the stable."

And, with the happy thought of a new lie, he turned to the stranger, who was following him in a rage, and said, —

"I did not understand, monsieur. The boy has taken them all to the stable, it was so cold."

"Took them to the stable! Why did he not take mine to the stable? What do I care for other people's horses? I will groom my own!"

And, with little comfort, Jean Gravier was left to take the rage of the drunken sergeant.

But this rage, and the rage of the two officers, who abetted and applauded the threats and abuse of their chief, need not be written down. Jean Gravier bent before the storm, acknowledged that it was natural that his guests should be indignant, but explained that they were wholly mistaken. He repeated eagerly his lie that the horses were in the stable, praying to all the saints in the calendar that they might prove to be so. In a moment more, he was relieved from the necessity of inventing any more lies by a shout from Andre, who appeared in the roadway, leading out four of the five horses from behind an old mill, which stood perhaps a furlong along the Lyons road, in the direction exactly opposite that which Antoine had taken.

Ah me! if Antoine had dared ask the stranger if he met five horses saddled, he would have gone the right way when he did go wrong; he would have found the horses; he would have brought them back undetected; he would have given Lulu her ribbon on Christmas day, and would have worn his own fine clothes. And now the poor boy is flying, as if for life, across the meadows.

Andre came leading along the coffle of horses. For a moment no one observed that there were but four, and should be five; but, the moment he came to the tavern with them, the loss of Cœur-Blanc was evident.

"It is that damned horse-thief from Meyzieux!" cried Jean Gravier, the tavern-keeper; "and he has stolen the best horse of them all." And Jean Gravier went sadly back into the tavern, to think what lie he should invent to satisfy the quiet gentleman with white hair who sat behind the door.

But, as the reader knows, the quiet gentleman with white hair had taken leave long before.

All this time he had been increasing the distance between him and the tavern as rapidly as Cœur-Blanc's longest stride would take him. The sun was yet more than half an hour high, though he had lost certainly half an hour in that miserable altercation, and in the enforced delay in the tavern.

At the moment when he found himself free, he had not mounted Cœur-Blanc; he had only cut the long halter at the place where it was fastened to the house, and by it had led along the five horses together, as if to the trough where they were used to be watered. If any one within the room heard their tread, he supposed the stable-boys were leading them to the trough, and to the cover which, as evening drew on, they all required. As the other horses drank, John of Lugio mounted his own. Not losing his hold of the halter, he walked carefully two hundred yards or more into the shelter of a little copse and of a deserted mill. Here he stopped, eager for time though he was, and once more securely tethered them all. Then was it that he gave Cœur-Blanc his head; and for the next fifteen minutes he rode like the wind.

He understood then, what the reader understands, that the troubadour, whose salutation he had acknowledged, but whose call he had not regarded, had been acting as his true friend, in an emergency when he had no other.

The man was one of the affiliated "Poor Men of Lyons." That was made certain by the signal he had given.

He had recognized John of Lugio, but in that uncertain way that a minute had passed before he was sure of his man. Then was it that the good fellow had been certain that the priest, whom all the "Poor Men of Lyons" loved and honored, was riding into danger; and then was it that he had turned and hailed him, in the hope that he might in time save him from the inspection and inquiry of the officers, whom the troubadour had passed just before at the tavern. In truth, he had gladly evaded them himself; for the reputation of the Lyonnais officers was so bad that any man of peace was glad to keep out of the way when it was in his power.

And now, as Father John saw, the good fellow had boldly come to the rescue, and had taken the chances of sharing his fate, that he might also take the chance of coming to his relief.[1] The priest did not dare think he was safe himself till he crossed the long bridge. But he heard no outcry behind him; and every minute, as Cœur-Blanc flew, was two or three furlongs gained.

Fortunately the high road was, for a while, quite clear of passengers; so that the tremendous rate at which he rode challenged but little attention.

Fifteen minutes may have passed before he dared take a pace less noticeable; and by that time the spires of Lyons were in sight in the distance. He satisfied himself that the sun was still high enough for him to pass without challenge at the drawbridge. And then, still keeping up a bold trot, he joined with one and

[1] This is no place for an essay on the troubadours or their poetry. But the author may be permitted to say in a few words, that they are not to be dismissed, as they are perhaps too often, as if they had no important place in the rapid changes and curious development of the time in which they lived. Every new manuscript disinterred and edited in France tends to raise rather than lower the estimate which is to be formed of their power and their merit.

It has already been said that the earliest specimen of their written language which we have is a Scripture poem, and that they were largely occupied in giving a general knowledge of Scripture to the people. In this regard they rendered, perhaps, more efficient service than their successors, to whom we give a French name also, — the "colporteurs."

Mr. Hallam says, "No romances of chivalry and hardly any tales are found in their works." But since Mr. Hallam wrote the "Middle Ages," many of the troubadour books have been discovered and edited. Among them is this curious Aucassin and Nicolette, of which I have transferred the beginning without hesitation to my story; because the critics assure us that the earlier versions of it belonged to the twelfth century.

Mr. Hallam's estimate of the troubadour poetry is in these words: —

"Their poetry was entirely of that class which is allied to music, and excites the fancy or feelings rather by the power of sound than any stimulancy of imagery and passion. Possessing a flexible and harmonious language, they invented a variety of metrical arrangements, perfectly new to the nations of Europe. The Latin hymns were striking, but monotonous; the metre of the Northern French unvaried; but in Provençal almost every length of verse from two syllables to twelve, and the most intricate disposition of rhymes, were at the choice of the troubadour. The canzoni, the sestine, all the lyric measures of Italy and Spain, were borrowed from his treasury. With such a command of poetical sounds, it was natural that he should inspire delight into ears not yet rendered familiar to the artifices of verse; and even now the fragments of these ancient lays, quoted by M. Sismondi and M. Ginguené, seem to possess a sort of charm which has evaporated in translation. Upon this harmony, and upon the facility with which mankind are apt to be deluded into an admiration of exaggerated sentiment in poetry, they depended for their influence. And, however vapid the songs of Provence may seem to our apprehensions, they were undoubtedly the source from which poetry for many centuries derived a great portion of its habitual language."

Mr. Pater has published an interesting essay on this little romance of Aucassin and Nicolette. He says: —

"Below this intenser poetry (of Provence) there was probably a wide range of literature, less serious and elevated, reaching by lightness of form and comparative homeliness of interest, an audience which the concentrated passion of those higher lyrics left untouched. This literature has long since perished, or lives only in later French or Italian versions. One such version, the only representative of its species, M. Fauriel thought he detected in the story of Aucassin and Nicolette, written in the French of the latter half of the thirteenth century, and preserved in a unique manuscript in the national library of Paris; and there were reasons which made him divine for it a still more ancient ancestry.

. . . "The writer himself calls the piece a *cante-fable*, a tale told in prose, but with its incidents and sentiment helped forward by songs, inserted at irregular intervals. In the junctions of the story itself there are signs of roughness and want of skill, which make one suspect that the prose was only put together to connect a series of songs, — a series of songs so moving and attractive that people wished to heighten and dignify their effect by a regular framework or setting. Yet the songs themselves are of the simplest kind, not rhymed even, but only imperfectly assonant, stanzas of twenty or thirty lines, all ending with a similar vowel

another group of those who were going into the city, and even ventured to chat with some of them as to the festivities which were in preparation. The Chapter was giving more distinction than ever to Christmas celebration, perhaps to signalize the advantages which the people of Lyons and the neighborhood were to gain from the new arrangement of affairs, which made them temporal masters of the city and suburbs, as well as their spiritual guides.

Father John felt a little sheltered when he rode chatting by the side of a well-to-do farmer, who was coming in by invitation to spend the holiday with his brother in the city. In front of them was a rude cart, covered with canvass, in which were the farmer's daughters and his wife. The talk fell, as it always did, on the crusade; and the man showed ignorance of the deepest dye as to its geography and its causes, which the priest did his best to enlighten.

"And will the knights be back, with the heathen hounds by Easter?"

"The good God knows," replied the priest, reverently.

"Yes; the good God knows, but what do you think? They have been gone long."

"It is a long journey," said the priest.

"Not so long, though, as those fine Englishmen had come, I suppose?"

"O," said Father John, surprised a little, "much longer!"

"Longer than they had come? Why did they cross the sea at all then? Why not go by land?"

Father John explained that England was on an island; that if the king of England left his dominions at all he must cross the seas.

"And do King Saladin, and the foul fiend Mahomed, — do they live on another island? I believe," said the stout farmer, "I should have gone to the Holy War myself, if I could have gone by land."

Father John exclaimed again that the Holy City was not on an island; that it could be reached by land.

"In the old war," said he, "many of the knights went by land. They rode their good horses all the way. But so many perished that the kings have taken ship this time, to go thither more quickly."

"O!" cried his friend, "they are all wrong. Many men would go by land who never would go by sea. I am one. Philippe there is two. Jean, Hubert, Joseph, — I could tell you seven men who would go were there no sailing."

The priest listened kindly, but the pace to which the good farmer held him was such that he dared not loiter long. He bade him good-by, and pressed on, to join one and another group of people, who were attracted in the same way to the city.

But always he was expecting to hear the challenge from behind of the Viguier's officers.

The last obstruction of all was, as he waited in a corner of the road, that a company of a hundred or more

sound. And here, as elsewhere in that early poetry, much of the interest is in the spectacle of the formation of a new artistic sense.

"A new music is arising, the music of rhymed poetry, and in the songs of Aucassin and Nicolette, which seem always on the point of passing into true rhyme, but which halt somehow, and can never quite take flight, you see people just growing aware of the elements of a new music in their possession, and anticipating how pleasant such music might become.

"The piece was probably intended to be recited by a company of trained performers, many of whom, at least for the lesser parts, were probably children. The songs are introduced by the rubric, 'Or se canto,' 'ici on chante,' and each division of the prose, by the rubric, 'or dient et content et fablioient,' 'ici on conte.'"

mounted soldiers might march past him, who were the men for whom his persecutors had ridden in advance, that they might provide their quarters for the night at Meyzieux. The priest waited till the last of them had gone, and then boldly crossed the causeway over the meadow before they came to the temporary bridge, where he was to pass the Rhone for the last time, — the bridge which poor Prinhac had crossed so fortunately in the morning. The sun was glowing, red and angry, above the height of Fourvières, and Father John had again so far relaxed the rate of speed to which he had held the horse, that his more decorous trot did not attract the attention of the town-servants, who were farmers' boys, and were going out of the town that they might enjoy the festival of the next day at their fathers' homes, or that of the groups of peasants who were pressing in to see the great solemnities by which the chapter celebrated the Saviour's birth, and amused their subjects at the same time. There were, indeed, so many of these parties now, and they proceeded at a rate so confidently slow, that, had the priest any doubt whether he should find the gates open, the number of travellers would have reassured him.

At the bridge itself, there was not even the pretence of any examination or detention. So many of the towns-people and of the peasants were passing in or passing out, that it seemed to be taken as an exceptional day, when the usual forms of military order might be relaxed, and the sentinel, who was lazily sitting on a bench by the portcullis, with his halberd lying by his side, did not so much as challenge the passers-by. Father John, who had heard from Prinhac the story of the secret of his passage, looked rather curiously into the face of this man, and of his officer also, who was lounging in the guard-house behind him. But he recognized neither of them. They certainly were none whom he had known among the clients of his "Poor Men of Lyons," and probably both belonged to some hireling company of soldiers whom the chapter had imported from another province.

The priest had picked his way across the bridge slowly and with caution, and now entered upon ground where every house was familiar to him, and had some story of grief or joy in his old memories. The streets were more alive than usual, because the Eve of the Festival of Christmas was almost as much a holiday as was the Christmas day proper. And Father John was well aware, that, had he been dressed in the proper uniform of his profession, any fifth person he met would have recognized him as one of the proscribed men. Recognition was dangerous at the best; but to night an arrest by some officer of the Viguier would make delay long enough to defeat any hope of his rendering the service he had been sent for. He had therefore, in the little distance left to him, as he threaded the streets of the town, a greater risk to run than he had incurred the whole day through. His risk was his patient's risk, and he must avoid it as best he could.

The priest looked eagerly among the groups of people who were gathered at the street corners, in the hope that there might be some one known to him as belonging to the affiliated "Poor Men of Lyons," whom he should dare withdraw from the crowd by a signal, who would take the well-known horse he rode quietly to its master's stables, while he himself found his way to the house on foot, and so escape observation. But the handful of the "Poor Men" who were in Lyons did not care much for such street gatherings, nor, indeed, were they greatly interested in such celebrations of Christmas as the Abbot had prepared. The priest was obliged to turn from the public square into a narrow by-street, less crowded with curious idlers. He dismounted from his horse, and led him by the bridle, and so approached a group of boys who were lounging in the open gateway of a tradesman's court-yard. He held out a copper coin in his hand, and said, "Which of you will take my horse across the little bridge for me? This is for him."

"That is not your horse. That is Messer Jean Waldo's horse, and no one rides him honestly, but Jean Waldo or his groom."

This was the impudent reply of the largest boy of the group. And all of them seemed, not indifferent to his money, but afraid of the errand. To be found with a stolen horse, as Lyons was then governed, might cost any boy his Christmas holiday, and, very likely, more.

The priest's imperturbable balance did not leave him. "It is Jean Waldo's horse, and it is to Jean Waldo's stable that I ask you to take him. Do I not pay enough?" Here is another of the Archbishop's croziers. And he took out another piece of money.

The bribe was a temptation. But the fear of the Courier was stronger; and the second boy answered, with a coarse oath, that the traveller had better take his own horses, and groom them too. And both these precocious young rascals, as if they were compromising the dignity of Lyons by so long talk with a dusty countryman, then gave a loud battle howl known to the other gamins of their section, and rushed wildly to the square, from which John of Lugio had just now turned. Two smaller boys, who made the rest of the group, seemed disposed to follow them, when the priest, perhaps because he must run some risk, perhaps because the purer faces of these boys attracted him, bent down, and said, almost in a whisper, "Could you take this horse to Jean Waldo's 'for the love of Christ'?"

"I will go anywhere," said the brave fellow, clambering into the saddle, "when I am summoned

'In His Name.'"

"You are to say, boy, that he who was sent for is close at hand."

"I am to say, that he who was sent for is close at hand. Farewell."

The boy was gone; and the priest, through court-yard and arched ways where he could not have ridden, hastily crossed the peninsula, crossed the bridge which spanned the narrower river of the two, and, in two or three minutes after the boy had given warning of his approach, he met Giulio the Florentine at Jean Waldo's door.

CHAPTER VIII.

CHRISTMAS EVE.

The master and his pupil fell on each other's necks, and kissed each other without one word. It was five years since they had met, and communication by letter or by message was most infrequent. And then the first words of both were for their patient.

"How does she bear herself?" These were the priest's first words.

"She is living. At least I can say that. I do not know if I can say anything more. At every hour her pulse is quicker and weaker, and her breathing worse. But there are now hardly any of the convulsions of agony. Do you remember that night with the boatmen at Anse? This girl has suffered as those men did not suffer."

"Does she know you?"

"She knows no one, and no thing. But she talks now to her 'dear mountain,' now to some old lame beggar, now to King Saladin, now to her cousin Gabrielle."

"She is living over the life of the hour before she took the drug. That is the way with these poisons"

These few words passed as they entered and crossed the court-yard, and mounted the stairway to the poor sufferer's pretty room.

In that day of the infancy of medical science, the distinctions among poisons now observed were quite unknown, even to the most learned. Poisons are now distinguished as irritants, narcotics, narcotic acrid, or septic, according as they act, by one or another method of injury on the human organization. The wild hemlock-like parsley, which grows abundantly in the meadows of Southern France, and which had been so carelessly substituted for some innocent root by Goodwife Prudhon, is one of the poisons known as narcotic acrid. In the eagerness of Mistress Waldo to make her preparation strong, she had even let the powder of the root itself remain in her decoction; and the child, in her conscientious desire to do all her mother wished, even because the medicine was so nauseous, had, alas, drank all the drugs of the preparation, as well as the more innocent liquid. The Florentine would be called only an empiric by the science of to-day; that is to say, only a person who acts on the remembrance of the results of his observations. He would himself have confessed that he was little more But his observations had been wide and intelligent. Since he was a child, the laws of life, and the methods of life, had fascinated him. And what he had seen of sickness and of health he had noted with absolute precision, and he had remembered thoroughly. When he wrote to his master that he suspected that the women had mixed one of the poisonous mushrooms of the valley of the Rhone in with their hemlock-brewing, it was because he had already detected symptoms, which were not to be accounted for, by the mere action of the root which he had identified in the mother's stores. These anomalous symptoms had, through the day, asserted themselves. And the Florentine, as it would seem, had varied his treatment somewhat from that with which he began. None the less, however, was the patient sinking. The balance and force of her admirable constitution, and her life of perfect purity, asserted themselves all along. But every symptom showed that she had less strength with every hour.

John of Lugio came to the bedside, and received silently, with a kind smile, the eager and profoundly respectful salutation of the child's father. Jean Waldo was surprised indeed. It seemed that this master of the young Giulio, this man so much hoped for and longed for, in this day of agony and of prayer, was one of those daily companions of his kinsman, Peter Waldo, whom he had, fifty times, seen with him at his home or at his store-house. For all of those companions, Jean Waldo's contempt had been even more bitter than that with which he regarded his kinsman. For he looked upon these men as being the tempters who lured the merchant into the follies outside his vocation. And now, as God ordered, it was this very man for whom he had sent his servants and his horses, for whom he had defied the law of Lyons, and for whose coming he had been hoping and praying all that day!

Madame Waldo rose from her chair at the bedside, and yielded it to the stranger, with a respectful courtesy. But, for a minute, no word was spoken in the room.

The new physician did not put his chilled hand upon pulse or forehead. He bent his ear close enough above the child's heart to listen to her faint breathing. He tried to catch the odor of her breath as it passed from her nostrils. He brought the candle closer to her that he might note the complexion of her face; and even threw it upon the open and rather rigid eye, which looked upon him so unnaturally.

Then he turned to his pupil, and asked in detail what he had tried to do for her.

The reader knows something of this already. Madame Waldo and her neighbors knew enough of the not mistaken medical practice of their time, to give to the suffering child full potions of oil stirred in with hot water as soon as they found that she had swallowed poison. Nor had they been unsuccessful in relieving her stomach from much of the decoction, and from a part even of the dregs of the draught which she had taken. But, as Giulio had found, the root and whatever was mingled with it had so long lodged themselves in her system, that the poison was, in a measure, absorbed by her organization; and the convulsions which made her father and mother so miserable, were the proof that they had not succeeded in removing all or most of the cause of her suffering.

"The convulsions never lasted long," said the young man to his master, "but they left her deadly pale, her face all haggard, and they came again as if we did nothing. Once and again I found it hard to open her mouth, so firmly set were her jaws. I have been all day long keeping up this warmth and rubbing, on which the women had begun. Her pulse seemed to me so exceptional, that at noon, and again three hours after noon, I ventured to draw blood, which we have saved for you to see. It is here. And it is now six times, at intervals of an hour perhaps, that I have given to her this bone-black which I had ready. I made it myself by the burning of sea-gulls' bones, and I know that it is unmixed, and that there is no vegetable in it. But whether it has absorbed anything, I dare not say. I have hesitated about giving wine to one from whom I was drawing blood. But when I could hardly find her pulse, and could hardly see her breath upon the mirror, I gave her Bourdeaux wine, such as you see here, and it seemed to me to do no harm. I renewed this twice therefore. And I have given her also, three or four times to-day, this camomile which her mother has served for me."

The Master nodded sympathetically, in approval or in assent, and, when his pupil showed to him the camomile, drained the bowl himself. He returned it to Dame Waldo with a smile, the first smile which any one had seen in that room for twenty-four hours, and the first indication which he had given that he was not wholly discouraged by the situation. The mother at least was encouraged. The new physician had thus entered on his work at that point, which is by no means the least important of a physician's duties, the care of the family of his patient. The good woman suddenly recollected that a man who had ridden fifteen leagues on a winter day, might be in want of some refreshment, and, only delighted that there was anything that she could do, retired instantly to her maids and her kitchen, to do what she then reflected she should have done before, and take order for his evening meal.

John of Lugio himself crossed to the open fireplace, and sat opposite the blaze, warming his cold hands over the embers. He asked the young Florentine one and another questions, called, himself, for the barks and leaves which the women had used in their pharmacy, and which still lay on broad salvers in a little antechamber. So soon as he was sure that his cold touch would not chill the girl, he went back to the bedside, assured himself as to the circulation in her feet and hands, listened at the beating of the heart, and noted the wiry pulsation of her wrists, and then with his own hand poured into the silver cup five times as much of the wine of Bordeaux as his pupil had dared to use. He then administered the whole draught to the girl, with a practised hand, and a sort of command in his manner which, even in her torpor, she obeyed.

"Do not disturb her. Let her lie," he said. And they both withdrew again to the fire.

"You relieve me more than I can say," said the young man. I have been haunted all the afternoon with the remembrance of Gerbert's axiom—"

"Which you have had the good sense to violate. Perhaps the child owes her life to your rebellion. The Pope Sylvester has learned something since he wrote out his axioms, and you and I must not be frightened by dead popes more than by living ones.* Your stimulant has done her no harm that I can see. And if she is to rally, we must help her if we can. Let me see your hamper there, and let us be ready to follow up your treatment with some elixir a little more prompt than my good friend's sour wines."

The blackamoor drew to the side of the fireplace a small table, and with his master's help brought from the basket a varied collection of flasks and bottles, which he set in order on it. The master looked at the labels on these in their order,—sometimes unstopped a flask and poured a few drops into the hollow of his left hand, and tasted them, set aside two of the phials, and then bade the black repack the others, and take them all away. Then turning to Giulio with a renewal of the sweet and half-quizzical smile, which had lighted up his face when he drank off the potion of camomile, he said, "Have you gone back into the dark ages? I have not seen such medicines since our great Bernhard died, because he had no better. I should think we were Adam and Eve in

* Gerbert, distinguished as a French naturalist, was afterwards Pope Sylvester the Second.

Paradise, and that Adam drank what Eve brewed."

"Dear master," said the Florentine, "remember where you are, and, first of all, speak lower. We are in the Dark Ages again, and, under the shadow of this cathedral, we are in the darkest centre of the dark ages. Why, my dear master, to speak of Averroes in any presence where one should be reported to the Courier, would be to sign the order for one's own exile to your mountains. And, though I might speak of Abulcasis, it is because no one in Lyons but yourself has ever heard of his name. No, we are to live and die by Eve's simples, exactly as we are to be saved or to be damned by Pope Alexander's theology. I have hoarded my essences and elixirs, drop by drop. And the little phials you have set aside here, are all that are left of the stores I rescued, the day when the tipstaves of the Viguier emptied your workroom into the street. I would fain have carried away your precious alembics, but the Archbishop's men were before me, and they all went to the palace."

"To the palace?"

"I suppose they went to the palace; perhaps they went to the dungheap; perhaps they went as a present to Muley Pasha. There is not a man in Lyons outside this room who knows their inestimable worth, nor how to handle them!"

"To the palace?" said Father John again, quite regardless of his pupil's last words, and almost as if he were dreaming himself. "To the palace! yes; to the palace!" Then he turned to Madame Gabrielle, who came in gently, and placed on the disencumbered table at his side a salver covered with a napkin and crowded with warm drinks, savory soup, and meat hot from her broiler. "I hope your worship is not faint," she said.

"My worship is better," he answered, with that same tender smile, "because I think that your darling here is no worse. Such prayers as you have offered for her, and, I think, such prayers as she has offered for herself, are profiting her well, and such care as you and my friend have given her this day, are fit companions to such prayers." As he spoke these gentle words, none the less did the physician-priest turn to the potage which the good dame had prepared for him. And he ate it with the appetite, not of a scholastic, but of a hunter or a soldier. As he ate, he went on in his talk with the Florentine, wholly regardless of the presence of the mother, who stood with her napkin on her arm as if she were a servant, noting every spoonful and every salt-grain of his hasty repast.

"To the palace, you say — to the palace! Do you mean to tell me, Giulio, that there is nobody here who cares for the Eternal Truth of things? Is there nobody who cares for the way God made the world? Where are all the old set — Lambert, Etienne, Suger, Montereau, Marly, and le Laboureur — where are they all? And your friends, the 'sacred five,' as you youngsters called yourselves? Alas! I answer my own question. Étienne and Marly were dead before the bad times came. Lambert and Suger are in Bohemia with our friend, because these people here know not The Truth, and The Truth knows them not. Montereau, they told me, went to the Holy War. He will come back, knowing something more perhaps. Would God they all had gone thither with as noble purpose!"

"And le Laboureur, sir, has burned his books and broken his instruments, and joined the Benedictines yonder in Cornillon. Of the sacred five you asked for, I only am left to tell you. George is under the Mediterranean. Hugh is with the Emperor, the others are at Acre, I hope, — they are in the East, as I had wellnigh been myself this day.

"No, my master; Lyons, I tell you, is the darkest spot of the Dark Ages."

The nurse at the bedside spoke at this moment, and the priest crossed to his patient. The child was more restive, and her stomach seemed likely to reject the draught which he had given her. He gave to her mother some direction as to her position, and the clothes upon her stomach, and, with quite another tone, came back to his pupil. "Give her thirty drops from this," he said, giving to him one of the reserved phials upon the table, "but it is a sin that we must poison her with sour wine, when we want to give her an elixir. Do you tell me that if love will not give us two hundred drops of the Elixir of the formula of Arnauld or Abulcasis, money will not do it? Has no man flask, phial, jar, or nutshell filled with it?"

"No one, my master, since the tipstaves broke into the warehouse of Simon Cimchi, and poured his precious elixirs into the gutter."

"No one," repeated the other, slowly; "no one except — in the palace. The archbishop knows his right hand from his left, and knows an elixir from a decoction. He has gone on the fool's errand. Who is in his place?"

The Florentine was not expert in ecclesiastical matters, and called Jean Waldo himself, who had sat silently at his daughter's bedside, to put to him his master's question: "Who holds the primacy of Lyons in the archbishop's absence in the East?" Giulio would have said that morning that, whether it were one priest or another, it mattered nothing to him.

Jean Waldo replied respectfully, that Father Stephen of St. Amour was the dean of the chapter, and acted as the archbishop's substitute. But he said that he was now absent in Burgundy on a visit with his family, and that the senior canon, one Father William, held his place. Jean Waldo knew that it was he who took the archbishop's place in the high solemnity of Christmas.

"William of St. Bonnet, perhaps; William of Roux, perhaps; William of Chapinel, perhaps; William of Cologne, perhaps. I remember them all, and there is not one of them all but will know my sign-manual. Giulio, will you take a message to this *locum tenentem*, this archbishop *pro tempore?*" And as he spoke he wrote rapidly on his tablets.

"You would not dare, my master?"

"The child's stomach will not bear your watery wine. But all the child wants is as much stimulant within as you have been giving to her skin without. In the archbishop's medicine-chests are doubtless my precious elixirs, and Cimchi's, I do not doubt, as well. If the archbishop himself were here, there would be no danger. He can handle an alembic as well as I can.

"As for daring, boy, to the child of God there is no danger. I came here 'for the love of Christ.' 'For the love of Christ' I shall bid this servant of Christ send to this child this elixir. You will not refuse to go, he will not refuse to give; if then the Lord pleases to give his blessing to our stumbling endeavor, all will be well. At the least, we will do our best, and make our endeavor

In His Name."

The Florentine said no other word, but rose, bowed, and took the parchment. There was written there this missive: —

For the Love of Christ.

To my Brother William, Canon in the Cathedral of St. John:

I write these words by the bedside of one of your flock, the child Félicie Waldo. The child is dying because we need for her the Elixir of Cordova, of the second formula of Abulcasis. Send it to us, my brother,

In His Name.

Your brother in Christ,
Jean of Lugio.

And at the bottom of the letter was the rough design of the cross of Malta.

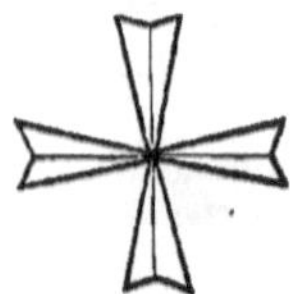

Giulio the Florentine took the letter, crossed the court-yard, and, as he went, threw over him the black student's gown, which he had left in the hall as he came up to the ministration which had held him here all day. He was amazed, himself, at the confidence with which he undertook an office so strange. Had anybody told him he was to go on such an errand, he would have said that the errand was absurd, and that success in it was impossible. But now that he had it to do, the confidence of his master gave him confidence, — nay, even the absolute necessity of success made him sure that he should not fail. It was clear that the master thought that unless this Elixir of Cordova could be found, and found soon, their battle was lost; that the child would not rally unless some stimulant could be used, more precisely adjusted, and more highly concentrated than any he had had at command.

On the strangest duty, therefore, as he knew, that ever he had been engaged in, the student left the weaver's court-yard; but still with the certainty of success. A few steps uphill, and he was within sound of the evening chant, as in the newly-finished nave of the Cathedral church of St. John, the whole chapter and the great company of subordinate priests were engaged in the first of the series of services of the great festival. The nave itself, the porch and the street in front, were crowded with people, and the young man saw that entrance there was impossible. He passed round the church to a little side portal, which gave entrance to a vestry which adjoined the chancel, and there he pressed for entrance.

He did not find it difficult to enter the room itself. For in the general enthusiasm and general confusion, all the minor clergy, and all the attendants and sacristans, of one tribe and another, had passed up to doorways and other openings, where they could see the pageant within, — and the Florentine soon found himself in the back of this throng, one of a crowd of half-official spectators. He chose his man instantly among these, and chose, as it proved, not unwisely. He whispered to a tall priest, who stood looking over the heads of the crowd in front, and spoke to him in that dialect of rustic Latin which was already passing into Italian in his own country. It proved that the priest was, as he suspected he was, his countryman, and understood him.

"I need," whispered Giulio, "to speak, at this moment, to his reverence the Dean."

"Impossible!" said the other, amazed at his presumption; "you see it is impossible. Yonder is the acting Dean in the Archbishop's chair. A moment more, and he will advance to the Eagle."

"Apud homines hoc impossibile est; apud Deum autem omnia possibilia sunt," replied the bold Florentine, still in a whisper. "It is impossible with men; but with God, all things are possible." The good-natured priest turned, with surprise, to see what man he was who quoted Scripture so happily and reverently.

"I tell you, my friend," persisted Giulio, eagerly, "I tell you I have that for the Canon William to see which is life and death, — perhaps for him, for aught I know,—certainly for others. He will not thank the man who keeps me away from him!"

"Who keeps thee away!" said the other, almost with scorn. "Enter if you can. You see it is impossible, at least for you and me. Hush, now, hush, you see he is kneeling at the Eagle."

The Eagle was the gilded Eagle, on whose outstretched wings lay the beautiful missal book, from which the Senior Canon, in place of the Dean and the Archbishop, was about to read his part in the service. With a clear and earnest voice he began.

"For the love of Christ, my friend," said Giulio, speaking almost aloud to his companion, "let us press in together. We two can reach his reverence with this missive. What is there that two of us cannot do if we attempt it

In His Name?"

The eagerness with which he spoke, in truth, and the invocation which he used, swept the other away. Scarcely knowing what he did, scarcely knowing that he exercised authority upon those that stood around, the father touched one and another of them, with command, as if he also had a part in the appointed service,— as, indeed, he had, if ever any man had special part in sacred ritual. So decided was his manner, that those in front of him instinctively obeyed. To his own surprise, and to Giulio's indeed, they were standing, in a moment more, in the front rank of the crowd of clergy who were looking in reverently upon the solemnity. The Florentine, at the instant, was inspired. One of those great impulses seized him, which do not often come to a man in a lifetime, — when he is swept away by a Life and Power larger than his own, and acts without fear or hesitation, though on a stage which he has never trodden before, and in a scene to which he has never looked forward. Taking his unknown guide by the hand, Giulio boldly walked across the brilliant chancel in face of the immense assembly, passing confidently among the kneeling priests, who were in their several places, till he came to the Eagle, and to the side of the Arch-Canon William as he knelt there. The priest instinctively fell on his knees at one side, while the student knelt on the other. To the clergy, each in his appointed place, this movement was of course inexplicable, and it was a surprise. To the great body of the assembly, however, it was equally inexplicable; but it was no surprise.

To them it was only a part of the great pageant, of which all the solemnity impressed and awed them, while they did not pretend to know the purpose of its several details.

The acting Archbishop himself was not aware of the neighborhood of these two new-comers. Completely carried away by the spirit of the service in which he was engaged, scarcely conscious of the presence of any of those around him, simply eager to carry to the multitude before him the true sense of the Scripture he was reading, and in his heart praying all the time for Divine Help that he might so render those sacred words that, even in this ancient Latin, these people might, in a measure, understand their import, the good father passed from point to point of the lesson, and only paused for the interludes which had been arranged to be played on the great organ, whose notes in this new-built Cathedral were still a novelty. The priest on one side, and the Florentine on the other, offered no interruption to his sacred service.

But, in a moment, the prelate had finished his reading, and the "organists of the Hallelujah," four priests who sang, in parts, a portion of the mass arranged for them, took up their service. As the prelate, awed by the solemnity of his own words, lifted his head from the bent attitude in which he had been reading, the Florentine touched him lightly on the shoulder, and said to him in Latin: —

"It is 'For the Love of Christ' that I am here and speak to you. A dying girl needs your help, and I am bidden to come to call you

In His Name."

There was not a priest of the lesser degree in the great circle around, but was chafing with indignation and amazement as he witnessed the utterly unauthorized intrusion which had been made in the very crisis of the great solemnity. But to William, who was the central officer in it all, whose whole heart was glowing with one eager wish that this people might understand how a child born in a manger might yet be the Prince of Peace, how the Lord of lords and King of kings might yet minister in the humblest offices, it seemed in this interruption as if the Holy Spirit had sent the immediate present answer to his yearning prayer; and when, in the language of Holy Writ itself, with the great invocation which had worked all miracles from the beginning, man spoke to him, he answered immediately, —

"Ecce adsum Domine"; and, to the Florentine, he added, "quo ducas sequar," — "Lord, I am here; where thou leadest, I will follow." At the moment, seeing the priest Alexander at his other side, he counted his presence also as a part of the vision or miracle which surrounded him; he touched him, in turn, and pointed to him the place of the reading on the open missal-book on the Eagle; intimated to him that he was to go on with the service when the organists of the Hallelujah were done, and so followed the Florentine out from the brilliant chancel, threading his way among the kneeling ranks of the amazed clergy, and came with him into the narrow crypts of the darker vestry. A crowd of officers of the church, from sacristans up to canons, of those waiting at the doors, turned and pressed around them; but their chief waved them back to the chancel. "Leave me alone with the messenger," he said, "and let the service of Nöel not be abated, not in one syllable of the office."

Then he turned to the Florentine, and almost whispered to him, "Adsum et sequar,"—"I am here, and I will follow."

"Your grace need not follow," said the young man, who was only surprised that he was not surprised at all that was passing. The truth is, that any actor in one of those waves of inspiration, in which true men are buoyed up together by the Holy Spirit, only feels that the whole is entirely what must be and should be; and his only wonder is that such strength and simplicity are not the law of all life. "Your grace need not follow. If your grace will read this message, that is all."

Father William glanced at the scrap of vellum which the young man gave him, looked from the top to the bottom, saw the invocation "For the Love of Christ," and the appeal "In His Name"; saw the signature of the old companion of his novitiate, John of Lugio, and saw the Cross of Malta, the significance of which among the initiates he well knew. The awe, which had controlled him from the beginning of the appeal made to him, was not diminished as his eye caught these words. He still felt that he was under Sacred Guidance, and read the letter once and again.

"O, my brother!" he said, then, with a sad sigh, "our brother asks what I am powerless to give. If our brother Stephen of St. Amour were here, he understands the Archbishop's alembics and elixirs. Even William of Cologne has some novice's notion of them. But I—I am but a child—nor do I even dare open the cloister room where these things are, lest I wake spirits that I cannot lay."

"If your worship will pardon me, I have studied of these elixirs with the very men with whom the Archbishop has studied." In that sacred presence, the Florentine would not name paynim sounds like Abulcasis and Averroes. "If your grace will only lead to the cloister, I will decide. 'Ecce adsum, quo ducas sequar,'" citing his own words of the moment before.

"As the Lord will. 'For the Love of Christ,' I do what you bid me. And service cannot be mistaken, which is rendered 'In His Name.'"

So saying, the prelate took from the sconce one of the large consecrated candles which furnished the light to the dim vestry, and bade the student take the other. They left the room in darkness, and, with these strange flaring torches, they crossed the court-yard to the amazement of the grooms in attendance, and entered by the Archbishop's private door to the corridor of his apartments, to the equal astonishment of the porter on duty there. The palace of the Archbishop was one of the grandest and most beautiful buildings then in France. As the young man stood in the magnificent hall of entrance, he wondered at the richness and beauty of its sculptures. After a moment's pause the Canon joined him again, coming out from his chamber with a heavy bunch of keys, and led the way to the corridor to the very end. He quickly turned the key in the lock, and said to Giulio, with a sweet smile,—

"To this moment. I have believed that I might be in a dream—nesciebam rem veram esse quod fiebat per angelum, sed putabam me visum videre." *

* "Nor deemed that it was true which was spoken by the angel, but thought I saw a vision."

"We are both guided by angels and archangels whom we cannot see, my lord." This was the young man's reverent reply.

The heavy door of the Archbishop's private laboratory swung open. The Canon himself, who had unlocked it, had never entered the chamber before. And the man of science was himself surprised, when he saw how extensive was the apparatus of mystery and of alchemy which was collected there. He recognized one and another implement of infant chemistry, which he had himself used in his master's workshop, and which the Archbishop had rescued from destruction when his master fled. He saw also in an instant that, as he had supposed, the stores of the Jew Cimchi had found their way to this collection. The place itself, with its collection of unknown machines, had a little of the look of that curiosity-shop, represented by Albert Durer, some centuries later, in which his weird Melancolia sits brooding. In the Archbishop's den, however, neither prelate nor physician had time to lose. The young man cast his eye around, and, seeing an exquisite cabinet of Venetian inlaid work on one side, asked his companion if there were no Venetian keys upon the chain which he had brought with him. A few experiments threw open the little case, and a series of choice phials — some of silver, some of glass — stood before them both, which the younger of the two visitors recognized at once as being of the most careful Saracen workmanship of the time.

He brought his tall candle to the little shelves, and read the names marked upon the several elixirs, tinctures, spirits, and "humors." To his eye, some of the flasks before him were worth a king's ransom. But at this moment they had not kings to ransom, but Félicie to save. And, in an instant, he showed to the prelate what they wanted. Marked first in Arabic, and beneath in Latin, was the "Elixir of Cordova, of the second formula of Abulcasis."

"Your reverence sees that here is what we need. Am I to take the flask to the child?"

The prelate bent, and read the second inscription. "It is in his grace's own handwriting," he said. "How strange that these Saracens whom we are riding down in the field are those who send to us the elixirs of life in our homes. Let it be as the Lord wills. If my Lord did not deem the elixir precious, he would not have saved it. But it is written that the paynim also shall serve. 'Ask of me, and I will give thee the heathen for thine inheritance.' Take what is needed, my son, 'For the Love of Christ,' and may the Holy Mother give the blessing which is promised to those who serve

'In His Name.'"

Unconsciously the father had twice used the first and last passwords of the initiated Poor Men of Lyons. The proficient started as he did before, when he heard the two phrases together, and felt, indeed, that the true minister before him had used them wisely and well. The permission once given him, he took the precious flask from its companions. The prelate locked the cabinet, locked the door of the cell, and then offered to go with the other to the child's bedside. "I will administer extreme unction, if you think her case so desperate."

"My father, the child is unconscious. But, at the least, her breath will not pass away for hours.' You can be ill spared from yonder service. If, when it is over, she needs your care, you shall find me waiting at the door of the chapel."

And so they parted: the Florentine with the priest's blessing, the prelate with the other's thanks. With his great candle flaring, he crossed the street in the darkness, passed rapidly up to the great cathedral door, and bade the throng open, that he might enter. At the sight of the great chief of the whole solemnity in his full robes of ceremony, the crowd in street and porch rolled back reverently, and the holy man, still wondering at all which had passed, walked up the nave, where all made room for him, bearing his flambeau still, and as if he were in a dream. To the multitude, this seemed a part of the ceremonial. To the canons and the other clergy, it was all amazing. He came to the altar as his humble substitute was chanting the words, —

"The glory of the Lord shall be revealed, and all flesh shall see the salvation of our God."

And never had those words seemed to Father William to mean so much as they meant now. He knelt at Father Alexander's side. He gave to him the candle which he bore, still burning, and assumed again his part in the Sacred office.

And so the service of triumph went on, the Communion and the Post-Communion. And, at the close, Father William offered the prayer: —

"Grant us, O Lord, we pray, that we may live in the new life of thine only begotten son, in whose heavenly mystery we eat and drink this night. Through that same Lord, we offer our petitions."

And it seemed to Father William that never had he known, as now, what that New Life was. And as, upon his knees, he thought how a Gospel of Love was lifting Félicie from the dead that night, and who should say how many more of the sick and suffering, the priest felt as he had never felt before, on the Vigil of the Nativity, that "the Lord had visited his people."

CHAPTER IX.

CHRISTMAS DAWNS.

The blackamoor was waiting at the outer doorway for the Florentine's return. The master, he said, was in Madame Waldo's kitchen, and thither the young man carried to him the precious Elixir.

"Thank God that you are here!" said his master who, with his outer garments off, was at work as a cook might be, over the coals. "And thank God again, that you have this that you are sent for." He held the dark-red elixir to the light, and smiled graciously and sweetly again, as he saw its perfect clearness and the richness of its color. "Dear child, these sour watery wines would not lie upon her stomach. You were right in using them so sparingly. I left her just now, after another of these spasms you described to me. I do not know but I myself brought it on. Yet I could not have seen her die before my eyes, in lipothymy, for want of stimulant and reaction. Now we can quicken the beating of her heart, without flooding her stomach with sour grape juice.

"My faith began to fail me. I knew she was lost if they had seized you," he continued, as they mounted the stair. "I was at work with the dame's pipkins and pans trying to make a little spirit pass over upon the bit of earthenware you saw me holding. But it was a poor alembic I had made, compared to that in which this spirit was distilled."

And so they entered the child's room once more.

The Florentine was amazed, himself, to see how much she seemed to have withered away since he was gone. He had been in that chamber twenty-seven hours continuously, before he left it. From minute to minute he had watched her face, and so gradual had been the decline which that time had wrought in it, that, from the very watchfulness of his care, he did not enough appreciate it. But the hour of his absence had changed her terribly. And because he had been absent, he now noted every detail of the change.

Ready for his use, John of Lugio had three or four silver spoons lying heated on the hearth, close to the embers. With a gloved hand he took one of these, dropped into it what he thought enough of his precious Christ-sent elixir, partially cooled it, for an instant, on the surface of a full cup of water, and then poured the spirit with a firm hand between the close lips of the child, who never seemed to struggle when he dealt with her. Jean Waldo, from the other side of the bed, and Madame Gabrielle, from the foot of it, sadly watched the whole.

The adept placed his hand upon the heart of his patient, counting the pulsations with his eyes closed, and then, crossing the room, set Giulio's pendulum again in motion. There stole over the girl's face an expression which all of them construed as that of relief from pain. No one of all those watching her said a single word, as a space of time which might have been five minutes went by. But in that time the dear child twice turned her head on the pillow, as if she would say, "I can sleep now," and her whole expression certainly came to indicate the absence of pain. The Florentine once and again renewed the motion of the pendulum; and his master, again by the bedside, as often noted the pulsation of the sufferer's heart, and counted the heaving of her lungs.

He said nothing. None of them now said anything. But at the end, perhaps of ten minutes, not dissatisfied, as it would seem, with the experiment, he heated again a few drops of the elixir, and again poured them into her mouth, which opened now without any of the spasmodic struggle which had, sometimes, checked their efforts for her. The master put his hand upon her forehead, smiled with that tender smile which they had now all come to look for and hope for, and then whispered to her mother, "Now for your hot cloths at her stomach and hot water for her feet again. If she sleeps she shall do well. 'Si dormit salva erit,' he said to Giulio again; "there is better authority for that than for any of Pope Sylvester's maxims."

And then, rather in following his example than in obedience to any formal directions, they all seated themselves, — the two physicians by the fire, the father and mother by the sides of the bed, the one attendant in the corner, and no one spoke a word. The last thing had been done that their skill or energy could command. Every one of the group had done, in his best way, what he could in bringing it about, and every one of them knew that now life or death was, in no sense, in their hands. In his own fashion, probably, each of them prayed: even the poor silent blackamoor, to such God as he knew; the mother, to the virgin and St. Félicie and St. Gabrielle; the father, with a wretched consciousness that he had hitherto conceived that his wife and daughter could do all the praying needful in that house, or that he could pay for what more might be needed; the Florentine as to the Spirit of Life, that that living spirit would so purify and quicken the child's spirit, that flesh and blood, drug and poison, might obey its requisition and command; and the priest, because the wisest of them all, with the very simplest prayer of all, "Father of all of us, come to us all."

There was no method of noting the passage of time, unless they had counted the beatings of their own hearts, now that the pendulum of the Florentine had been left unmoved. But, after a longer space than any, in which either the girl's stillness or their own anxiety had permitted them to sit silent before, the master crossed to the bed again, felt of her head and of her heart again, and then, with his pleased smile, nodded to his assistant, and, in a whisper, bade him bring a larger draught than they had given of the cordial. He only nodded and smiled, as he caught the anxious and eager, questioning look of Madame Gabrielle. But those signals were enough, — and she, poor soul, was on her knees at the bedside, in the most voluble prayer, though wholly silent.

The master indulged her for a few moments in these grateful devotions, then walked round and touched her on the shoulder, and made her supremely happy by summoning her to duty. It was simply that she should place a fresh pillow on the bed, and then, with her stoutest maid, should lift the child from the one side of it to the other, that she might have the best chance for the sleep which seemed now to be nature's best restorative. These cares ended, he banished Madame Gabrielle absolutely from the room, and her husband as well. He bade the maid prepare a bed for the Florentine, as if he were her master, and sent them both away. He told the blackamoor to renew the heap of wood by the fire, and then to wait in the corridor till he was called. He extinguished all the candles which they had been using in their several cares, so that he could remove from the girl's bedside the screens which had kept the light from her eyes. And then, as the only watchman by the flickering fire of her earthly being, he threw himself into one of the deep arm-chairs which Madame Gabrielle had provided, and, in the absolute stillness of the night, waited the issue of their efforts and their prayers.

As he looked into the waning embers of the fire, and saw, once and again, a spark running in its wayward course, up and down and everywhere on the back of the chimney, telling what the children called prophetic tales to the looker-on, — as he looked back, were it only on the events of that day, since he was interrupted by the charcoal-dealer, as he compared the various readings in St. Jerome's Evangelistaries, but just before noon, it was as if in to-day's experience his whole life took order before him. The master was not much in the habit of raking over the embers of his past life, but it was almost impossible not to look into them in the midst of the reminiscences of such a day as this.

Of the two Benedictines whom he had met so unexpectedly by the postern gate of the abbey at Cornillon, one was the companion even of his childish life, the son of his father's nearest neighbor. The master's memory did not go back to a time before that, when, with a little boy of just his own strength and size, he dug in the sand-heaps by the road-side, or made ineffectual traps for the sparrows. With that boy he had grown,—had worked in the simple farm-life of the fields around Lugio,—had, when they were older, learned his letters, and learned to write at last. The parish priest had taken a fancy to both these boys, who discouraged the noisy and mischievous urchins of the town, as they all sat together in the church, and wondered when the mass would be over. As the little fellows grew bigger, the worthy man selected these two to be robed in little robes, and to carry, in the service, bell and book and incense. He loved nothing better than to walk with them and talk with them, now of saints and their battles and victories, now of birds and snakes and frogs, or of flowers and fruits, as they found them in the fields and woods and marshes. And, by this selection of his, and by their own natural bent, it had happened that, when the other boys around them became masons, or vineyard dressers, or sometimes carriers and merchants' men; when some of them went into the service of one or another of the neighboring gentry, and so showed themselves, on the first holidays, in new jerkins or hauberks, to the wonder of the boys less smartly dressed, Jean and François had too much to do in the service of the church, or in studying with the priest, or in one or another message of his, sometimes taking them as far as the Cathedral, and into high intimacy with archdeacons and canons; had too much of this dignified and grateful service for them to think or care for the more carnal lines of life in which their companions were engaging. François, his companion, under the ecclesiastical name of Stephen, was the older of the Benedictines he had met that day. It was in one of those early journeys, when he was yet hardly more than a boy, that he had gone on some errand to the great Monastery of Clairvaux, a place not unfamiliar to him, and had been actually there, awaiting the answer to a message, when the great Bernard died,—the man to whom all Europe deferred more, as it owed more, than to any other. And as the master looked back, he knew that it was the lesson of that hour, sad and solemn, which had determined him, then and there to give up his life to the service and help of other men. Then came on years of life,—impatient enough at the time, very likely, but, as he looked back upon them, sunny indeed, and crowded with incident and enjoyment. The sailing down the river with his lively companions, of which the Baroness of Montferrand had reminded him, was a fair enough illustration of that life. And there was a wrench at his heart now, renewing many and many a march of many a night of struggle at that time, as he asked himself now, for the thousandth time, *if—?*

"If he had then and there given up his determination to make himself a priest, if he had then and there asked his mother's goddaughter, Anne of Thoissey,—so brave and true and loyal as she was, and so beautiful withal,—to share life with him; and If—

"IF she had said, what it sometimes seemed that she might say; and they two together had given themselves to the service of God and ministry to man, might it have been that they could have rendered wider service, and made their own lives and other lives more godly, than had happened as it was?" He had torn himself from her, and with so many of these men, with whom to-day was mixing him again, had entered on his priestly training. And she, — at this moment she was abbess in the Convent of Montmerle. Was she happier and better — and was he?

Then there was all his earlier training of manhood, and the taking of his vows. And the memories of all those young men who then surrounded him: they were now canons and deacons and bishops and archbishops; they were with Philip and Richard in the East; they were the heads of houses here in the West; yes, — and so many of them were in heaven! How strangely had every one of them falsified every prediction which, in those days of their novitiate, they would have been sure to make regarding each other!

And so he came down to the period of a man's activity, to what one of our poets calls "the joy of eventful living." Those happy days here in Lyons, when he never looked back, and scarcely ever looked forward; when he found, at his right hand and at his left hand, noble men and noble women from every grade in life, only eager to serve God as God should show them how. The practical enthusiasm of Peter of Waldo! The discovery of new truth and higher Life which each day made, as they studied gospel and epistle! The strength they all gained in sympathy: sometimes from the droll beggars who came to them in travel; sometimes from women and children who seemed inspired in the very proportion of their ignorance of books; waifs and strays these, who came to light, as the "Poor Men of Lyons" assembled the troops from highways and byways, from hedges and ditches, at their houses of bread and houses of God! In the midst of this, as if it were almost another man whose life he was recalling, came the memories of all those studies in physical science, the fruits of which he was this night using; his journeys to Cordova and Seville; his interviews with the Cimchis and Abulcasis; the enthusiasm which even Guichard, now Archbishop, showed, as in the cell of Abulcasis he and Jean of Lugio together saw for the first time what seemed almost the miracle of distillation, and their first success in repeating that experiment with the humble apparatus which they two had made for themselves! And to think of what had passed since then! Guichard, an archbishop, Lord of the fief of Lyons, and John of Lugio, an exile, with a sword hanging over his head!

And so his memories ran down through all the days of trial. First, there was the happy work over Scripture with Peter Waldo, with Bernard of Ydros, and with Stephen of Empsa. Then, the journey to Rome with Peter Waldo, and the welcome by Pope Alexander, more than cordial — the welcome which gave such wings and such courage to their return. Then, John of Balmeis's scorn, as he received the Pope's letter, his pretended inquiry, and his bitter and cruel excommunication. Then, the wretched years of suspense, more wretched than those of certainty in exile; Peter's second visit to Rome; the council called by Lucius, and its jealousies; the clergy against the laymen, and the laymen scorned and rejected. "Ah me," said John of Lugio, aloud, "it is always as it was in the beginning The carpenter's shop could gain no welcome in the temple courts, and it cannot to-day. He was despised and rejected of men."

Had he disturbed his patient by speaking?

She turned on her pillow, and said, "Mamma! Mamma!"

John of Lugio gently crossed the room, removing the candle from its shelter as he did so, that she might see him distinctly, and then he said, as if he had known her all her life, and was her dear friend, "Your mamma is asleep now, dear child, and she has left me to take care of you. She left this bunch of grapes for you to wet your lips with."

"Bunch of grapes — wet my lips," said the girl, almost laughing at the oddity which supposed that she, of all people, needed nursing in the middle of the night; and then she tried to rise upon her elbow, and then found she had not just the balance that she needed, and dropped back upon her pillow. "Where am I? what is it?" she asked, more doubtfully.

"You have been very ill, my dear child, but you are better now; wet your lips with the grapes; that will please mamma; or let me give you a little of the broth which she left for you."

"Broth which she left for me? Did not I drink some — herb drink which she made for me? or — or — is that — all that — a horrid dream? O, sir, I have had such dreams." And she sank quite exhausted on the pillow.

"Dear Félicie, you shall forget them all Take mamma's broth, and take with it a little of this cordial, and try to sleep again." There was little need for persuasion. The child lay almost impassive as he fed her; thanked him then with the same prettiness and sweetness with which she spoke to beggar or worshipper on the hill or in the church of St. Thomas, and, in a moment, was asleep again. But sleep now was so beautiful and so regular, her pale face had lost so entirely the lines of agony and struggle, that the priest, as he looked on, thanked God in his heart of hearts for the greatest of blessings, the return of health, and for the sight most beautiful of all His gifts, — the sight of a sleeping child.

As he returned to his watch by the fire, the silence of night was broken by the chimes of the cathedral. In an instant more he heard the rival chimes of the Abbey of Ile Barbe, and then the chimes of Ainay, and then the ringing of bells that could not be named, as Sts. Machabees and St. Nizier and St. Paul, and the tower of the Augustins, and every church and abbey and convent in all the country around broke out with joy to announce that the Lord of Life was born into the world.

"Unto us a child is born," said John of Lugio, reverently.

Hour after hour his quiet watch went by. Wise as he was, he did not dream that only on the other side of the doorway, crouching on a mattress, through all these hours, was Madame Gabrielle, waiting for sound or signal which might give her permission to return to her post at her child's side. No! The house was so still, that the wise man thought that all had obeyed his orders, and that all were sleeping. From hour to hour he took such occasion as the child's occasional restlessness gave him, to feed her with her mother's broth, and to give the precious stimulant of the Archbishop's elixir. And she, dear girl, fairly smiled in her sleep, once and again, as happier dreams came over her, and as Nature asserted herself now, that the poison was so nearly gone from her. At last, as the priest supposed, this night had nearly sped. He drew the curtain, and he was right; there was a gray light spread over the east, in the midst of which the morning-star shone with beauty preternatural, with a light so bright that he could see it reflected in the river below. The light was so gentle that he thought it would not disturb the child. He crossed to the door to bid the black call Madame Gabrielle. And lo, she was already there! He led her to the bedside, that he might show to her the glow of new life upon Félicie's face. And just as they approached, the child opened her eyes again, and looked wistfully around, and even sat up and began to speak. "Mamma, mamma."

And he delivered her to her mother.

With that gift of Life new born, the Christmas Day of that home began.

CHAPTER X.

TWELFTH NIGHT.

When Twelfth Night came, the great hall of Jean Waldo's workshop had been cleared from all its looms.

In their places were three long tables, which stretched from end to end of the long room, and across the top a fourth table, which united these together.

All through the day the great kitchen was crowded by the eager servants of the household, and all the neighbors' kitchens were put into requisition as well, to furnish forth the most noble feast which had been seen in Lyons for many, many years. Men even whispered that the great feast, when the Archbishop entertained King Richard and King Philip, was not so grand.

That morning Félicie, and her mother and father, and her cousin Gabrielle L'Estrange, and many others of the family, — "too many for to name," — had all gone together in a little pilgrimage of thanksgiving to the cathedral. Félicie had begged that they would take her to her own little eyrie church of St. Thomas, on the top of the hill; but no, that was quite too far, even though Félicie rode in the chariot which appeared in public so seldom. At the cathedral, also, they could be present while the good Father William said mass, and their solemnity would hardly be complete without him.

After this offering, they had all returned together to the house, and there the grand salon was opened, the room which seemed to Félicie almost mysterious, so seldom did it see the light of day. And when it did, she found that it was like most other mysteries, for there was very little in it. But to-day, dear old Eudes, who had been a sort of major-domo, or servant-master, in Madame Waldo's household, even before Félicie was born, had done his best to make it seem cheerful. At each end a lordly fire, made of great oak logs, blazed cheerfully. Eudes had sent the lads everywhere to bring laurel and other evergreens to hang above the chimney-pieces and between the windows and around the sconces; and after they had come home from mass, when one and another of the guests began to appear, whom Jean Waldo had summoned from far and near, — as they gathered, at first a little shyly, around one fireplace or another, but soon unbending before the genuine hospitality of all who were at home, and as people will unbend, in France of all nations, when old and young meet in the same company, — the great hall was then cheerful indeed. The talk was loud and the merriment contagious. Dear little Félicie sat in a great arm-chair, with her feet lifted upon a footstool, but she did not look as if this care were in the least needful. Only her mother and her father seemed to feel that unless they were taking care of her, in some visible fashion, at every moment, all might escape again, and be gone. But Félicie had her aids, to fetch and carry for her, and to run hither and thither with her messages. She said she meant to play at being queen upon her throne; and, indeed, she was so, pretty creature, in the midst of all that assembly. Gabrielle L'Estrange took great airs as being a lady in waiting, and came and whispered, and ran hither and thither, as if her sovereign's commands were most difficult of execution. And for the first hour, that shy, pretty Fanchon, the daughter of Mark of Seyssel, stood almost constantly at the side of Félicie's chair. She was dressed in a holiday costume, such as the peasants of the hills were fond of wearing, so simple and pretty and quaint that she attracted everybody's notice in the midst of the Lyonnaise girls, in their more uniform costume. Fanchon felt at ease with Félicie from the very first kiss. It took her longer to adjust herself to Gabrielle's busy, active, diplomatic managing of the party. But Fanchon; also, melted at last to the simple courtesies and hospitalities of the place. And, as the afternoon began to come in, and the winter sun crept in a little at the western windows, Félicie had the joy to see all her guests — for her father said that this was her party, and only hers — obeying the sound of pipe and tabor and harp, and dancing merrily, from one end of the hall to the other. Always there was a little court clustered around her throne. But always she would order them away, in such couples as it pleased her Majesty to select, and send them out again "to try the adventure" of the dance, she said. "To try" this or that "adventure" was the standard phrase of the romances of the troubadours, with which Félicie and her young friends, and, indeed, all the company, were wholly familiar.

And, before the early winter sun went down, others joined in the festival, so that when Eudes came bustling in, to tell Madame Waldo that all was ready at the tables, Father John of Lugio was one of her guests again. And she brought him to her daughter, and, in that sweet, courteous way of his, he told her Majesty that he was bidden to take her to the supper-room, and asked her to lead with him the procession. And then, even to Félicie's amazement, and almost to her terror, Father William appeared also, whom she had not seen before, and Father William followed close on Father John, giving his hand to Félicie's mother. And then the order required that Giulio the Florentine should lead in Madame L'Estrange, who wondered indeed herself at finding herself so provided for, and then the other guests followed, in many a combination quite as strange. In a few minutes all were ordered: Félicie at her mother's side, and on their right and left the two priests; the Florentine and Madame L'Estrange; the Baron of Montferrand and the Lady Alix. Even the two monks, Stephen and Hugh, had obtained some sort of dispensation from their convent, and were here; Gualtier of the Mill was here; Mark of Seyssel and his wife and all his children, down to Hubert, were here; poor Prinhac was here, with his arm in a sling; the officer of the night, who threw up the portcullis so promptly, was here, and the sentinel who held the gate. Here was the farmer of the hill-side. Here was every groom that had cared for the horses who that day sped so well; here was the boy who rode Cœur-Blanc into the stable, when Father Jean was afraid to be seen; here was Father Alexander, who crossed the blazing chancel so fearlessly with the Florentine. Here was every messenger who had been sent on that sad night for Félicie's father and for the doctor; every neighbor who had brought in oil, or snow, or herbs, for her relief; every maid who had warmed a plate or filled a jug of hot water for her. More than seven score guests were assembled, of every degree, — gentlemen and grooms, ladies and scullion-maids. The invitations had been given with diligent care to every one who had done anything, in that night of trial, which had helped our darling Félicie, and to every one who had tried to do so.

Father William asked God's blessing on the feast; and, with great merriment and joy, it went forward. The young men and the girls had every sort of joke about the Twelfth-Night presents, which they had secretly brought for each other; and, at the last, there was great ceremony and rivalry as to who should have the sacred bean, which was baked in the Twelfth cake, which Félicie pretended to cut, and which was, in truth, cut by the strong right arm of John of Lugio. No; there was no manner of cheating or forcing, and the bean fell to the pretty Fanchon, — Mark's daughter, — who blushed almost as red as her own bright ribbons when Philip L'Estrange brought to her the bean on a silver plate, and made to her a low bow and a flourishing speech, in which he said that her Majesty Queen Félicie sent it with her royal regards to her Majesty Queen Fanchon. The feasting went on, and the fun went on, and no one seemed to enjoy the feasting or the fun more than Jean Waldo himself, though he sat at neither table, but passed about from guest to guest, with a napkin on his arm, as one of the servants, bringing here a plate, and there a cup, and urging all to eat and drink, and only happy as he saw that his guests were happy, and were provided for.

And, when the feasting seemed to be nearly ended, not because the bountiful stores provided had failed, but because there is an end even to a Twelfth-Night appetite, Jean Waldo came round, and stood by John of Lugio, and whispered to him, and then the Father rose, and asked for silence, which awaited him of course. And he said, nearly what I have said, that this was Félicie's feast, and that her father had given it for her, as his simplest way of showing honor to all who had prayed for her and toiled for her on the terrible night when her life was in danger. "He wants to thank you all, and to promise you his best prayers for your welfare in all your lives. He is afraid he cannot say what he would fain say," said the master, "and so he bids me say it for him to you all." And there was great clapping of hands from all the guests at all the tables, and they all cried "He is welcome, he is welcome," and some cried, "Long life to the lady Félicie." And poor Félicie was crying, as if her heart was breaking, though her face seemed so happy all the while. And her mother held her hand, and cried as if her heart was breaking too.

And then Jean Waldo waved his hand, and said, "I do not know how to speak as these Fathers do. But I must try. I must thank you all, all of you, with all my heart, that my darling is here, and that we are all so happy. Ah, my friends," he said, "you know me for a hard man, who has said to you a thousand times, that I would take care of my affairs, if other people would take care of theirs. O, my God, I have said it again and again,—I know not how often I have said it to those who are in this company. But I learned everything, I think, on the eve of Noël. In those terrible nights I learned that I wanted others—O, how many others—to take care of me and of my dearest concerns, yes, though they risked their lives for it, as my friend here did so bravely. And as those slow hours went by, I prayed to my God, and I promised him, that whether my darling lived or died,—whether she lived with me here, or with his angels there,—for me, I would live from that day forward for all my brothers, and all my sisters, for you, and for you, and for you; yes, for all his children, if I could help them. But, dear friends, I could not begin to do this, without asking him to forgive me, and you to forgive me, that so often I have said I would care for myself, if the others for themselves would care. I could not begin to live for the rest, without asking the rest to pardon me that I had lived for myself before. And so, at little Félicie's feast, I ask her, and I ask you, as I ask the good God, to show me how to take care for others, and to show others how to take care of me."

Some of the guests were weeping, and some of them were clapping their hands, and some of them were shouting "Long life to our Host, long life to Master Jean." But Father William, who was standing with the tears running down his cheeks, waved his hand; and they were all so amazed that he who acted as Archbishop should be here at all, most of all that he should sit and stand so near to John of Lugio, that they all stopped their shouting, that they might listen. And he smiled drolly, and as if he had a secret, upon them all, till he saw that all were very curious; and then, with his finger, he drew in the air the sign of the Cross of Malta; and then he said, "I will teach our brother how to forget himself, and how to live for others. What he does, let him do 'For the Love of Christ,' and whom he welcomes, let him welcome

'IN HIS NAME.'"

And then, passing behind Madame Waldo and little Félicie, he threw his own arm about John of Lugio's neck, turned him, all surprised as he was, so that he was face to face with him, and kissed him.

O, the cheering and clapping, the tears and the surprise! To those who were initiated, the wonder was how the reigning prince of Lyons had come upon their secret. To those whose eyes were only partly opened to what Jean Waldo had seen so clearly in those visions of his terrible night-watches, it was as if Saladin and Philip had kissed each other on the Mount of Olives. To those initiates, who were as bigoted in their way as was Montferrand, it was all amazement, that an Archbishop of Lyons, or any one who sat in an Archbishop's throne, should have any heart, or should speak aught but evil. To the churchmen, as to Alexander and Hugh and Stephen, it was relief unspeakable. For here was their chief, doing more than they had done to express sympathy and love which they were yearning to offer to all.

Jean of Lugio himself did not seem surprised. With an eager embrace he returned the embrace,—with a second kiss upon William's cheek, he returned the kiss. "Ah!" said he, "the Kingdom of God has truly come. The City of God is rescued, and we are in it now. Heaven can offer us nothing sweeter than we have here. You will never misunderstand us, William; we shall never misunderstand you. What you ask of us we shall perform; for you will ask 'For the Love of Christ,' and we shall answer

'In His Name.'"

CHAPTER XI.

THE WHOLE STORY.

My uncle Adrian had brought us home this story, which you have been reading, from the city of Lyons. He had walked over every inch of the ground that Félicie had tripped over, that Giulio and Jean Waldo had hurried over, that the Canon William had passed over as he bore his weird candle through the darkness; he had crossed the short bridge and the long bridge; he had seen the site of Jean Waldo's workshops; had climbed to the church of St. Thomas, which is now "Our Lady of Fourvières"; he had crossed himself there, and had seen there the fresh votive offerings, which young soldiers have hung there, whom our Lady saved from wounds in the Prussian war. My uncle had looked across the valley of the Rhone, to see the distant Mont Blanc near thirty leagues away.

He had been through those Dauphin Mountains, and the scarped hills to the north of them; down the valley of the Brevon and the Alberine, and along the Rhone, crossing it back and forth, twice, just as Father John of Lugio did. He would not say that he had found the charcoal hut of Mark of Seyssel, but he would say that he had been on the place where it might very well have been.

Then he had spent a happy day, how happy, in that quiet but cheerful old library at Lyons, where nobody cared about Peter Waldo, but where all were as ready to serve my uncle as if he had been Henry Fifth himself. He is about the age of the Fifth Henry. And here he studied Claude Francis Menestrier's ponderous civil or consular history of Lyons, while the full-length portrait of the benevolent Claude Francis Menestrier smiled on him from the wall above. He studied Montfalcon's Monuments of Lyons, magnificent in its apparel and precision. And was it, perhaps, M. Montfalcon himself, who showed such courtesy to my uncle, though his French was so bad, and he a stranger without introduction? Then he studied pamphlet upon pamphlet of indignant men who had to reply to M. Montfalcon for this and for that, for which this reader need not care, so that my uncle well understood that the flame which Peter Waldo and John of Lugio, and the other Poor Men of Lyons, lighted, was not a flame which burned out in one century, nor in two, nor in five. Nay, when my uncle went into the street, and found that the City Council were trying to lock out the Government Prefect from their own old town hall, he thought the old flame seemed to be burning still.

And many a map of brook and river and mountain had my uncle brought home,—and many a sketch and photograph which we have not shown to you. He had many a story of those who befriended John of Lugio and Peter Waldo, in their time. And long stories he had to tell us of this hidden valley, and that defended cave, in which one or another of the Poor Men of Lyons, or of those Waldenses, who, for centuries after, defended the same faith, had hidden; but these things had nothing to do with our little Félicie's Christmas and Twelfth Night, so that, as my uncle writes out her story for you, they are not written down.

It was on two warm September evenings, as we were all at the New Sybaris, by the sea shore,—two of those evenings when we can have every window open, but when, so early is the sunset, there are two or three hours after tea before it is bedtime,—it was on two such evenings that my uncle read to us the story of Félicie, of Jean Waldo, of Giulio the Florentine, of the ride to the hills, and the charcoal-burner's hut, of John of Lugio, and of Christmas eve, as poor Félicie spent it, and as the Canon William spent it; and then of Christmas morning, and of Félicie's Twelfth-Night Feast,—the story which you have just now read, dear reader, to which you and I give the title,

"In His Name."

My boy Philip had been permitted to sit up later than usual, to hear the end of the Twelfth-Night Feast. When it was finished, his mother bade him take his candle, but he lingered a moment to ask his uncle the inevitable question, "Is it true, Uncle Adrian?"

"I do not know why not," said my uncle. "Peter of Waldo was driven out, just thus and so, and John of Lugio with him,—two men of whom the world was not worthy. Richard and Philip went to the Crusade just there and then, and broke down the bridge as the story tells you. Averroes and Abulcasis, and a dozen others like them, had, just then, set every man of sense in Europe on the studies which turned the old quackeries of medicine upside down. And the 'Poor Men of Lyons,' and their associates in the mountains, had to protect themselves with all their wits, I can tell you, and with more passwords than the story tells you of, as they went back and forth from city to mountain. Which Canon William took the dean's place when he was away, the story does not tell, and I do not know, but it was some Canon William. Whether Cœur-Blanc's feet were white or black, the story does not tell, and I do not know; nor whether Mark's daughter Fanchon were fifteen or sixteen. But this is true, I am sure, that none of them in the end failed who did anything 'for the Love of Christ,' if they could find anybody to join them 'in His Name.'"

"My dear Philip," said his Aunt Priscilla, "there has been just the same story going on in this last week, here under your nose, only you have been too busy with your boat and your gun to see it or hear it."

"Going on here, dear aunt?"

"It is always going on, Philip. Jesus Christ is giving life more abundantly, and awakening the dead now, just as he said he would. When Dr. Sargent gets up at midnight, and rides behind the old gray twenty miles before morning, to poor old Mrs. Fetridge's bedside, do you suppose he does it because he thinks the town will pay him half-a-dollar for going? He does it because Jesus Christ bade him do it, though very likely he never says he does it 'for the love of Christ,' or 'In His Name.' When Mr. Johnson sent down the mustard that I put on Mary's chest last night, sharp mustard and fiery, instead of sending saw-dust, colored with turmeric; do you suppose he did it to save your father's custom? He did it because he would rather die than cheat any man out of the shadow of a penny. And that comes from what your Father John would have called 'the love of Christ,' and working 'in his name.' Or when the expressman came in afoot last night, with the telegram from Kingston, when his team had broken down, because he was afraid it was important, do you think he walked those five miles because anybody hired him? He did not make any cross of Malta, and he did not speak any password at the door; but, all the same, the good fellow did his message for 'the love of Christ,' and never would have done it if he had not lived and moved, his life long, among people who are confederated 'in his name.'

"Five hundred years hence, dear Phil, they will publish a story about you and me. We shall seem very romantic then; and we shall be worth reading about, if what we do is simple enough, and brave enough, and loving enough, for anybody to think that we do it 'for the love of Christ,' or for anybody to guess that we had been bound together

"IN HIS NAME."

www.ingramcontent.com/pod-product-compliance
Lightning Source LLC
Chambersburg PA
CBHW020042030726
47499CB00007B/2539

* 9 7 8 3 7 4 1 1 9 2 0 1 2 *